Hiding
with the
Billionaire

BILLIONAIRES OF REKD BOOK 1

Hiding
with the
Billionaire

from AWARD-WINNING author
DONNA K. WEAVER

Donna K. Weaver

Emerald Arch Publishing

EMERALD ARCH PUBLISHING

Hiding with the Billionaire

Copyright ©2018 by Donna K. Weaver

Edited by Katharina Brendel, Portable Magic Editing Services
Cover design by Steven Novak | Novak Illustration
Author photo by Sherry Ward of SW Portraits

ISBN Paperback: 978-1-946152-12-1
ISBN eBook: 978-1-946152-11-4
ISBN Audiobook: 978-1-946152-13-8

Printed in the United States of America

Donna K. Weaver's author website is www.donnakweaver.com.

To my sons who introduced me to the world of Esports.

Hiding
with the
Billionaire

BILLIONAIRES OF REKD BOOK 1

Gaming

Chapter 1

In spite of the warmth of the Arizona spring, Ahri Meisner held her cold hands to her chest, fear battling frustration, as her husband frantically threw his clothes into a suitcase.

"What's going on, Zed?" She kept her voice level. When he was like this, it never helped if she showed her emotions. "Where are you going this time?"

"It's business." He refused to look at her, which wasn't a good sign and shot her anxiety even higher.

Ahri had never seen him so agitated before, and that was saying a lot, considering how Zed had been acting lately. What had he gotten himself into? She wished for the time when he'd have trusted her with it, when they'd first married. They'd told each other everything back then. The way he'd started pulling back from her had been gradual, subtle. She hadn't recognized it until he'd taken the new job last year.

"Why won't you tell me anything?" She stepped closer.

"It's better if you don't know."

Better if she didn't know? She watched him grab his socks from his dresser and toss them into the suitcase. It was like she was staring at a stranger; she didn't feel like she knew him at all anymore.

Last year, when he'd started working late or attending meetings out of town, she'd thought it was just the new job. She'd tried to get him to talk about what he was working on, but he would always turn secretive. Why? He was a certified public accountant. It wasn't like she was asking for client information.

That had been when she'd first considered that there might be someone else. The thought had paralyzed her for a while. Was this what her mother had gone through, seeing the signs and watching her husband pull away from her, unable to do anything to stop it?

Finally, in desperation, Ahri'd asked Zed straight out if he was seeing someone else. He'd told her to stop being stupid. His response had been so indignant, so *honest*, that she'd believed him. The confrontation hadn't stopped his secretiveness though or kept him from moving into the spare bedroom.

They'd stopped going out, both as a couple and individually with friends. It was like they existed in two bubbles within a bubble, excluded from anyone who'd once mattered to them and separated from each other.

With Zed out late at business meetings or away on business trips, she'd sat home alone as a distraction from her pathetic life and played the game her brother had helped create. The few friends she'd had left hadn't been able to talk her into going out with them.

She'd floated in a kind of limbo, unable to fix her marriage but refusing to move out, not after what her father's leaving had done to her mother. Once upon a time, Ahri and Zed had been friends, and friends didn't run out on each other.

"Have you done something illegal?" she asked.

Zed zipped up the suitcase and faced her. Her throat went dry at the anguish in his expression.

"Please tell me," she whispered.

"We're done." He picked up the bag, seeming to steel himself, determination closing him off from her with a finality so firm it was like he'd turned a key in a lock. "I'm leaving, and it's not safe for you to stay here either."

A cold chill went down Ahri's spine. It seemed like she was standing on the edge of a cliff that had started crumbling underneath her, and she was about to plunge into the chasm below.

"Why do *I* need to go somewhere?"

"Will you stop asking stupid questions?" Zed shouted. "I told you it's not safe. Can your mother take you?"

Take her, not stay with her. Ahri felt stupid, like her brain couldn't make sense of his words. He wasn't just going on a business trip; *he* was leaving *her*. How ironic since she'd been debating leaving him for six months.

"I can't go to her," Ahri said, raising her voice for the first time. "Don't you ever listen anymore? She moved back to Korea last month."

"Call your brother then." Zed didn't spare the sneer he always used whenever he mentioned Kayn. "He's got plenty of money to keep you safe."

There was that word again. Safe.

"Zed, please. Are you okay?" She reached out to touch his arm, but he jerked away.

"Don't you get it?" he hissed, the veins in his neck bulging and his expression crazed. "It's over. *We're* over."

Ahri dropped her hand and stepped away. She bit back a bitter laugh. It'd been over from the moment he'd taken that new job.

"It's been fun, but . . ." His words dropped off and he stared at her for a few seconds, his expression a myriad of emotions—sadness, regret, and something Ahri'd never seen there before. Fear. That was when she realized his hands were shaking as he walked away. Out of her life.

She didn't know how long she stared at the quilt on his bed, rumpled from his frantic packing. Still numb, she walked into his bathroom. He'd been in such a hurry he hadn't even taken his toothbrush.

Rafe Davis, CEO of REKD Gaming, stared at the computer monitor on his desk. Success might cause him to self-destruct like one of the champions from the battle arena video game that had helped to make him and his partners all billionaires. How could something that had seemed so incredible at the time have turned into a burden he didn't know if he could shoulder anymore?

His gaze shifted to the folder on his screen that held the emails his assistant had diligently filtered. Maybe two assistants weren't enough. He did have other staff members who carried a fair amount of his workload, but he wanted to spend more time working with the game's writing team. His MBA from Harvard made him the perfect partner for the administrative part of the job, and he did it well. He just *needed* more, the creative outlet his friends had.

Rafe rubbed his temples against the growing headache. Once their launch into the world of Esports was complete, he could take some time from his admin duties. Until it was, he didn't dare slack off. Their pro teams from various regions around the world were finishing up their spring splits online and then heading into the International Summer Invitational. REKD expected at least twice as many viewers worldwide as they'd had last year. It was going to be huge.

Glancing out the window, he took in the gardeners who were planting bright annuals in the flower beds. North Carolina had provided a mild morning, and one of the storyline teams sat outside, brainstorming. He wanted to be out there with them.

He let out a deep breath. As his mother was fond of saying, *there is no rest for the weary.*

"Rafe," Kayn called as he burst into the office, "I need your help."

"Mr. Rafferty," Rafe's assistant Olaf said, rushing in behind Rafe's partner and head programmer. "I'm sorry, boss. He wouldn't let me announce him."

Rafe raised a hand to indicate he didn't mind the interruption.

"I don't know what to do," Kayn said when Olaf had retreated from the office.

"Sit down." Rafe's headache ratcheted up. If Kayn's programming team had run into a problem, it could delay the update. "Tell me what's wrong."

"It's my sister."

Rafe blinked and then let out a breath. He'd met Kayn's sister many times when she'd visited Kayn at Harvard and later when she'd attended a few company events. She'd been pleasant, if a little quiet, probably overwhelmed by her older brother's good fortune. Pretty too. Rafe had found himself drawn to her unusual hazel-green eyes. He reminded himself that she was married.

"What's going on with Ahri?" Rafe asked.

"She's in some kind of trouble." Kayn sat on the edge of his chair, his fingers tapping nervously on his leg. It must be serious if he was this upset. "I've told you what I think of her husband."

"Has she finally decided to leave him?"

"Believe it or not, *he* left *her*." A flash of anger crossed Kayn's face. He jumped to his feet and started pacing. "It seems Zed's gotten himself into some kind of trouble, and he told her she needed to get away." He stopped in front of the desk, his jaw muscles working.

At the tone of his friend's voice, the hairs on the back of Rafe's neck stood up. The siblings were close, talking several times a week, but Kayn had never come across as overly protective. Was Kayn angry *and* afraid? Considering how much he disliked Ahri's husband, it could be the former, but why the latter?

Rafe leaned forward. "What happened?"

"She said she thought she was being followed on her way to work yesterday." Kayn started pacing again. "When she got home from work last night, already creeped out, she saw the police there. I guess a neighbor had scared off someone who'd broken into Ahri's apartment. It'd been ransacked."

Rafe rose and began pacing too. He wouldn't allow his reason for being so vested in Ahri's wellbeing to be anything more than because she was his friend's sister. It had nothing to do with him being interested in her even before she'd gotten engaged. She was married. Or had been. He gave himself a mental shake.

"And she didn't tell you about it until this morning?" Rafe asked.

"She said there's been a rash of break-ins, and the police thought it was random. Then first thing this morning, she saw the same guy who'd been following her hanging around outside her apartment building. That's when she called me. It's also when I found out Zed had left her the night before."

"You can't trust her safety to coincidence."

"I'm not going to. I have a mover coming this afternoon—had to pay out my teeth to get them to do it last minute." Kayn paused and rubbed his face, looking weary for the first time.

"Take the jet and bring her back with you," Rafe said, putting a hand on his friend's shoulder.

"I was hoping you'd say that. I know this isn't business, but I'll pay for the fuel and whatever else the accountants think is fair."

"Don't worry about it. You have plenty of room in your suite. Or, she can stay at my mother's."

"Boss?" Olaf asked hesitantly over the intercom.

"Good timing." Rafe took his seat again. "Kayn will need the jet ready in an hour for a flight to Arizona." He looked up. "Phoenix, right?"

"Yeah." Kayn shifted uncomfortably. "That's another problem."

Rafe straightened, a sinking feeling in his stomach.

"My team's right on the cusp of getting this right, and I'm in the thick of it."

"And you need to be here, or they'll have to wait until you're back."

"Yeah."

Rafe stared out the window and rubbed his temple again. A delay would cost them tens of thousands of dollars. He let out a breath. It didn't matter. Family came first.

"Then we'll roll it out late," he said.

"We can't. You've got all the marketing lined up." Kayn's voice turned hesitant. "There's another option— *you* go instead of me,"

"*Me?*" Rafe jerked his gaze back to his friend.

"I wouldn't entrust her to anyone else. I know you'll make sure she gets here safely."

"I don't know . . ." Rafe said, staring at one of his closest friends. He and Kayn had met while taking a computer class at Harvard. When Rafe had found himself overwhelmed, computer whiz Kayn had come to the rescue. They'd hit it off and been friends ever since, and he'd been there for Rafe when Tess had ditched him. He was flattered that Kayn would trust him with something this important, but didn't a distraught woman need her brother at a time like this?

"I already asked her if you could bring her back here instead." Kayn raised his hands at Rafe's expression. "I feel guilty enough, but she's tougher than you might think. When our father abandoned us, she's the one who kept us together. Our mother was an emotional mess. If not for Ahri making her pull it together, we'd probably have ended up in foster care."

"Um, boss?" Olaf said over the intercom.

"Hang on, Olaf." He glanced at Kayn. "You're sure she's okay with the substitution?"

"Her exact words were: Just get someone here right away." Kayn shrugged.

"All right then." Rafe reached for his keyboard. "Olaf, please clear my schedule for today and most of tomorrow. There's nothing on my calendar that can't be postponed."

"Thank you." Kayn was already backing toward the door. "I'll get back to work. I owe you, man."

"And don't you forget it," Rafe called after his retreating back before turning to the intercom. "Olaf, please order a car too."

"Already done, boss."

Rafe grinned. He doubted there was anyone as efficient as Olaf at this job.

"I need a suite with two bedrooms for one night. I've been wanting to check out that Phoenix gaming den anyway. I'd like to see for myself how people are liking our more recent updates."

"Good plan."

"And please see if Bill Ryze is available to come," Rafe added.

"Security?"

"It's a sensitive issue."

"Understood." Olaf hung up but then appeared at the office door, looking hesitant. "Um . . . I know this is bad timing, but there's something I need to tell you."

"Yes?" Rafe braced himself.

"I'm giving notice." Olaf's voice had gone soft, like he was a little kid who was having to confess something.

Rafe's headache spiked, his heart sinking. Cass, his other assistant, was expecting a baby soon and would be off work for the twelve weeks after. When Olaf had been placed on the waiting list for law school in the fall, Rafe had thought he'd have more time to find and train a replacement.

"I'm guessing a place opened up."

" *Yes.*" Olaf's excitement burst through his reticence. "I just found out last night. Since they're accepting me so late, I'm on a time crunch. I'm really sorry to just drop this on you."

"How much longer do I have you?" Rafe rubbed the bridge of his nose.

"Until the end of the week. I have to be on the road first thing Saturday morning."

"At least I'll be back in time to say goodbye before you abandon us." Rafe tried unsuccessfully to make it sound lighthearted.

"Ah, boss . . ." Olaf sounded sincerely regretful. "It's really been a pleasure to work for you. I've learned so much."

"Don't worry about it." Rafe *was* happy for the kid. "You'll make a killer lawyer one day. Now get to work."

"Okay, boss."

Rafe leaned back in his chair. Could it get any worse?

Chapter 2

"That was my mother's." Ahri hurried over to where a giant of a man had picked up the glass-enclosed Korean doll wearing a traditional Hanbok dress. She blinked against the tears that had been fighting to get free since Zed had walked out. Flaring her nostrils, she took a deep breath. She refused to cry over him; he didn't deserve it. "*I'll* pack this one."

"Whatever." The guy shrugged and moved to her china hutch to help a second man.

Yes, go break the china. I can replace that. Zed's horrid mother had given them that. Ahri gently picked up the foot-high glass case, wondering how best to protect it from breaking. It'd take a special kind of box and proper padding to protect the doll.

She clenched her jaw. If she'd had any idea she'd be moving, she could have started packing her few delicate treasures sooner, though she was relieved some had survived the break-in. She could also have given proper notice at work. How was she ever going to get another decent executive assistant job with that on her record? Quitting like this would leave them in the lurch, and they'd been good to her too, especially when things had started to go sour with Zed. Maybe she shouldn't—

That too-familiar sensation of being watched struck Ahri again, and she stilled. Her hands went clammy, memories flooding back of when she'd approached her apartment complex to find the police there, yellow tape cordoning off the area. For a second, panic had filled her. What if Zed had come back—and someone had killed him? But her fear had been for nothing; there was no sign her husband had been there.

Ahri carefully put down the glass case before her trembling hands dropped it. She tried not to be obvious as she straightened and arched her back like it hurt, glancing out the window as she did. A familiar looking middle-aged man slowly strolled across the street, watching her. As soon as she met his gaze, he dropped it, shoved his hands in his pockets, and hurried away.

The hair on the nape of her neck stood up. Her gut told her he was involved with the break-in. Hadn't he gotten what they wanted when they'd destroyed her home? Why was he still watching the apartment? Watching *her*?

She pinched her lips, forcing herself to breathe normally. Last night the police had taken down her information and then blown off her assertions that she was being followed. The officer who'd taken her report had been sympathetic, but she could tell from his expression that he'd thought it a random act. Right. Her husband had claimed it was dangerous to stay there, and it was just a coincidence that her apartment had been broken into the very next day.

For a second, she considered calling the police about the man but decided against it. They wouldn't believe her anyway. Ahri glanced out the window again. Besides, it looked like he'd left.

That morning, after a fretful night, Ahri had almost convinced herself that the police were right, that Zed's dire warning *had* made her paranoid. But when she'd looked out her window before dawn and seen that same man leaning against the lamppost and watching her building, she'd called her brother.

She pulled the curtain closed and went in search of a good packing box. The sooner she was out of here, the better.

By mid-afternoon, most of it was done, but she still hadn't found a box and packaging she'd trust for her mother's doll. She wondered if she could take it with her on the plane as her carry-on.

She went to a pile of things too damaged to fix and picked up a pair of jeans that had been slashed. Why would whoever had trashed her apartment cut up some of her clothes? It seemed so . . . *personal,* like someone was trying to send them a message. That was stupid though. Zed had to be the one they were after. She wasn't involved in whatever he'd gotten caught up in.

Thinking about it made her head hurt. How could her routine and boring life that included only her job, occasional lunches with coworkers, and visits to the gym have turned into this nightmare with a stalker who ransacked her apartment and shredded her clothing? Because she was sure the two were related.

"Oh, it's true," Taliyah's familiar voice cried.

Ahri turned and found her coworker standing in the apartment doorway. The woman was the mother of three girls and had been the only friend who hadn't allowed Ahri to push her away when things had gone bad with Zed.

"You poor thing." Taliyah strode across the room and pulled Ahri into a fierce hug. "Some of those cats at the office said you were making it all up."

"Seriously?" Ahri stepped back and surveyed the room full of broken possessions. One of the things she would *not* miss about her job was the interoffice bickering. The cliques had turned into warring factions. "I guess I should have known they'd act like this since the news only listed my apartment as 'one of several break-ins'."

"Oh, honey, where will you go?" Taliyah started to put her hand on Ahri's shoulder, but the woman's phone rang. She answered it. "*Yes*, I'll be back in a few minutes." She disconnected and heaved out a breath. "I had to run to the post office, so I came by to see you off. Call me when you get— Where did you say you're going?"

"My brother's making the arrangements, but I'll be in touch."

Kayn had been adamant that no one know where Ahri was going. The people at work only knew that she had a brother who was a computer programmer, not that she was related to one of the Harvard Billionaire Boys, as the press had labeled them.

"I wish I could stay longer. You take care of yourself." Taliyah pulled Ahri into a quick hug and hurried from the room.

Watching her leave, Ahri felt the rift from her old life. It was real. Sniffing, she bent to pick up a pair of ruined jeans and paused. The corner of a white photo album peeked from under a ripped blouse. She pulled it out. Their wedding album. She vaguely remembered tossing it over into the pile last night. Why hang on to pictures of a relationship that had died?

Ahri opened it and stared at them in their wedding clothes, so happy. Zed's tall good looks, especially his bright gray eyes, had captured her attention the end of their freshman year in college. They'd gotten serious quickly, even though his mother hadn't approved of him dating *that Asian girl*. Looking back now, Ahri wondered if a sense of rebellion had been part of the reason he'd been attracted to her.

As she studied the photos, it struck her how young Zed looked, so much more than he had the night he'd left. It was like he'd aged a decade instead of only three years.

Ahri flipped the page and blinked. Three photos were missing. She searched the other pages and even shook the album. The pictures were gone. Glancing around the room, she didn't see them. Had Zed taken them? No. He hadn't even remembered his toothbrush. Besides, he'd dumped her. Why would he want to take photos of them?

Her gut twisted. Had the person who'd done this taken them? She dropped the album and buried her face in her hands.

"We're here, sir," Bill Ryze said.

Rafe glanced up from his laptop and identified the building by the moving truck. The men carrying boxes from a second-story apartment meant they must be well along on the packing. He glanced at the driver.

"Privacy, please," Rafe said.

She nodded and a divider went up between the front and back seats. Olaf had outdone himself. The vehicle had the outside appearance of a large model SUV while the interior was like a limo. His assistant's sense of humor also played into the choice because it looked like the stereotypical black villainous cars used in action films. Rafe was going to miss that kid.

"Bill, you've had time to think about this weird situation, and I'd like your assessment."

"I read through the police report during the flight." Bill's gaze scanned from the movers to the other side of the street. "There were a number of other incidents in the general area, and the local police think it was probably a gang initiation or some teenagers being stupid."

"What do you think of Ahri's statement that she was being followed?"

"That I don't have enough information on it. She reported that her husband left the day before and with a warning that people were after him. I checked. Meisner is an accountant who quit his job last week, evidently something his wife didn't know. There's a chance that he's emotionally unstable, and his paranoid claims have frightened her enough to see things that aren't there."

"That's possible, I suppose."

Bill glanced at him with a frown. "But you don't think so?"

"There's the break-in."

"That could be a coincidence."

"Yes." Rafe watched the movers, feeling an urge to find Ahri and make sure she was all right. "But I don't think we should blow this off. I don't know her all that well, but Kayn talks about her a lot. Nothing I've seen myself or heard him talk about fits the description of a woman likely to fall prey to delusions."

"She might be emotional because her husband just left her."

The man's remark made Rafe cringe a little. If his mother had been there, she'd have had a hissy fit about it.

"That's kind of a sexist comment," Rafe said, "assuming a woman shouldn't be believed because she's overly emotional about something bad that happened to her."

"I wasn't suggesting she shouldn't be believed because she's a woman. My wife would kill me." Bill went back to surveying the area. "I'd expect Kayn to be emotional too if he were married and his wife had just walked out on him. Anyone would be."

"Fair enough, but this whole situation makes me uneasy, and I don't know why. I understand from Kayn that Ahri's very left brained. I don't think she's the overly emotional type. I can't see her getting so spooked that she's seeing bogeymen everywhere. I know I could be wrong. Sounds like she's been through a lot lately with her husband. That could mess with anyone's head." Rafe had an irrational desire to punch Zed Meisner for putting her through this.

"I understand, sir. I'd already decided not to discount her concerns. I've also decided to request that Kayn have the truck deliver his sister's possessions to a different location, in a different state."

"A different state?"

"If someone's after Mrs. Meisner, we don't want the truck to lead them right to her. I'll call Kayn about making the change while I check things out here."

Rafe nodded, his stomach knotting. He reached for the door handle. "I'll find her while you do that."

"Sounds good."

Rafe made his way up the stairs in between the movers and identified the apartment by the open door. He was about to rap on the doorjamb when he saw Ahri in the middle of a pile of stuff that must be meant for the dump. She held her face in her hands. His heart gave an odd twist. Maybe he *had* underestimated the emotional drain on her.

"Ahri?" he asked, striding toward her.

At the sound of his voice, she jerked up her head, her hands flying to her chest. Recognition washed over her face.

"Rafe!" She launched herself into his arms.

He staggered back a little, as much from surprise as from her forward motion. It definitely wasn't her usual way of greeting him.

"Hey." Rafe had to wrap his arms around her to keep them both from tumbling to the floor. "Are you all right?"

Ahri trembled and shook her head against his chest. He held her, rubbing her back, and making soothing sounds like he did when his younger brother or sister were upset, though holding her definitely didn't make him feel brotherly toward her.

"What happened?" he finally asked.

She took a deep breath and looked up at him. "They took pictures from our wedding album. Why would they do that?"

Rafe glanced at where she'd been standing. An elegant white binder lay open. He'd attended the wedding and recognized some of the people.

"Show me." He took her hand without thinking about it and led her to the pile. That was when he noticed the slashed and jagged tears on the clothing. His mouth went dry. No one had mentioned that. He'd need to let Bill know. And Kayn.

Ahri picked up the album, flipped some of the pages, and handed it to him. She pointed to the spots where three photos used to be.

"And you just now noticed these pictures were gone?" Rafe asked. "Could Zed have removed them some other time?"

She shot him a flat look.

"I'm just trying to figure this out." He shrugged.

"I'd been looking at it the night before he left as a reminder."

"A reminder of what?"

"Of what it used to be like." Ahri looked off in the distance, blinking her eyes. "To help remind me why I should stay."

When she self-consciously wiped at her eyes, he wanted to take her in his arms again. He resisted, though he did take a slow breath to calm himself. How long had she been unhappy in her marriage? The more he was hearing about the situation, the angrier he was getting with Zed. What had the man been thinking to hurt her like this? He'd had this smart, talented, beautiful woman—

Rafe shut down the thought. It wasn't getting them anywhere. He pointed to the empty spaces on the two pages.

"So, you'd just been looking through the album, and you know the pictures were there?"

"Isn't that what I just said? Do you think I'm making all this up too?" She glowered at him.

That was more like the Ahri he was used to seeing spar with her brother. It made Rafe feel a little better.

"Don't fly off the handle. I wasn't insulting you. I wanted to make sure I understood you right." He tilted his head and arched a brow. "It's a form of active listening."

"All right." She huffed out a breath. "Sorry I snapped at you."

"And there's no way Zed would have taken these."

"Why would he take our wedding pictures? He walked out on me." Her tone went flat, monotone. "He didn't even take his bathroom stuff."

"So, why would someone else take the pictures?" he asked softly.

"I have no idea." Ahri dropped her arms, weariness radiating from her. He wished he could do more for her.

"It looks like you're planning to toss this." Rafe held up the album.

"Why would I hang onto it?"

"I think you should keep it as a precaution—because whoever did this to your apartment wanted them." His instincts told him the missing photos meant something. If it'd been a random act, why steal the pictures? "Do you remember who the people were in the shots?"

"One was of me with my maid of honor and my bridesmaids. Another was of Zed and me, and the last one was me alone."

"So, *you* were in all of them."

Ahri turned those bright eyes to meet his, the tendons on her neck taut.

"Hey." Rafe brushed a strand of hair from her cheek, surprised at the tingle of attraction. "Don't be afraid. We have your back."

"Thanks." Ahri looked down and sniffed.

"Let's go. The car's waiting." He tucked the album under one arm. "I want to talk with my head of security about this."

"You believe me?" Ahri pressed her palm to her chest.

"Yes. It's obvious *something's* going on here." Rafe didn't want to upset her more, but the condition of the apartment unsettled him more than he'd expected it to. The idea that some ugly character was willing to trash her place—and do that to her clothes—made him anxious to get her away from here. "Since we have no idea what it is, I think we should enlist some help while getting you away from here."

"It makes me so mad that someone's trying to scare me, and I don't even know why."

"Same here," Rafe said. "Let's go."

"I still have to clean," Ahri said, "or I'll lose my deposit."

Rafe pulled out his phone and dialed the office, putting the phone on speaker.

"What's up boss?"

"Did you order a cleaning crew?"

"Of course." Olaf sounded insulted that Rafe had felt the need to ask. "They should be there by now, waiting for the movers to finish before coming in."

"Excellent as always. Please contact them and tell them to haul to the dump whatever is left in here. Pay whatever the fee is." He ended the call.

"I can pay my own fees." Ahri crossed her arms, reminding Rafe of his mother when she anticipated resistance to something she wanted done.

"Okay." When Ahri frowned at him suspiciously, like she expected an argument, he added, "I'll have Olaf send you a copy of the invoice. Now, why don't you check the rooms to make sure you haven't left anything."

She didn't say anything but turned toward the bathroom. While she was busy opening and closing drawers and cupboards, he flipped through the photo album. Her happiness showed through the pictures. Zed's behavior couldn't have been going on too long, or Kayn would have said something.

Unless Ahri had been hiding her crumbling marriage from her brother. It'd been bad long enough that she'd resorted to looking through the album to talk herself out of leaving. Like Kayn, she had some pretty strong opinions about people who walked out of a marriage.

Rafe did too, for that matter, though for different reasons. An image of Tess when she'd refused his ring flashed through his mind, and he pushed it aside. Sometimes you could think you knew someone and not know them at all.

"That's everything. Let's go." Ahri had her pocketbook over her shoulder and carried a glass box holding a doll in traditional Korean dress. She held her back rigid and barely flinched as she walked away from her old life.

Rafe's respect for her went even higher. He followed, still carrying the photo album.

Chapter 3

A hri blinked when she saw the interior of the SUV and stepped back to look at the exterior again before sliding into the seat.

"I'm impressed," she said after shutting the door.

"My assistant has a sense of humor," Rafe said.

A man Ahri didn't recognize took the front passenger seat, but Rafe didn't introduce him. The man seemed very watchful of everything around them as the driver started the car and pulled away. Was her stalker still around to see her leave?

"That guy who was following me yesterday was outside earlier today," she said.

The man in the front seat shifted to look back at her. "You should have said something about that when we first arrived."

"And who are *you*?" Ahri bristled, not caring that she was being rude. She was tired, emotionally frayed, and finished with people acting like she was the one who'd done something wrong.

Rafe reached over and touched her clenched fist. "He's Bill Ryze, head of my security." He shot a warning glance at Bill with a tip of his head toward the driver.

Mr. Ryze nodded and turned back to face the front, but his watchfulness seemed to increase.

Ahri relaxed her hands. Why hadn't Rafe introduced them earlier? Probably because this Ryze was keeping an eye on things outside. She wished she'd known about him earlier. She might have thought to mention the stalker, but he'd already gone by the time Rafe had arrived anyway. It wouldn't have mattered, right? Ahri was suddenly grateful for the darkened windows.

She glanced at Rafe. He fingered the cover of the album, looking pensive. Because he believed her? The little knot that had been growing in the pit of her stomach since the night Zed had left loosened a little. Rafe hadn't blown off what she'd said. He'd brought his top security guy, who seemed to be taking her information seriously, though maybe security people were just like that. Either way, she didn't feel as minimalized as she had even an hour ago.

Her mind drifted over how her life had changed so drastically in the last two days. Instead of going to her graphic design class tonight, she'd be fleeing the state. At least Taliyah already knew about it, so Ahri wouldn't have to cancel tomorrow's lunch date.

She leaned her head against the window, looking forward to getting on board the plane and not having to worry about being followed. It felt a little like she was one of those colorful little balls in that corn popper push-toy that Taliyah's toddler played with. Ahri's whole life had been turned upside down, and her mind just couldn't think beyond getting away from here.

She closed her eyes, fatigue weighing on her. Only when the SUV stopped did she open them.

"Wait. The *Biltmore*?" They were going to stay the night here? Ahri just wanted to get out of the state right away and leave the whole nightmare situation behind. She wanted her brother. "I thought we were going to the airport."

"It's been a long day for you," Rafe said as a doorman opened his door. "I have business in town I can take care of tonight."

She pressed her hands to her abdomen; she wouldn't get to see Kayn until tomorrow. Only then did she realize how much she'd been looking forward to it. She'd been counting on him to help her make sense of it all.

"Thanks for letting me know," Ahri snapped, surprised at the sudden burn in her eyes. She closed them, pinching the bridge of her nose; she *wouldn't* cry.

Rafe sat in silence for a second. "I'm sorry. I assumed you'd know we'd stay the night since it's such a long flight, and I've already made the trip once today. My mistake. Will you be all right?"

His words made Ahri feel like a selfish brat. He *had* dropped everything to come across the country to get her. She took a deep breath. No, she wouldn't overreact. She knew Rafe was being kind and not looking to hurt her feelings.

"I'm sorry. That didn't come out well." She forced her voice to sound light, "This is a beautiful place. I've always wanted to stay here."

"There's one in North Carolina too," he said, "but I've never been to that one."

The driver had the back of the SUV open, and a hotel staff member was pulling out their luggage. They were either very fast and efficient, or Rafe's assistant was and had called in advance.

Ahri followed Rafe inside with Bill bringing up the rear, feeling like a poor second cousin in her grubby jeans and T-shirt, while Rafe and his security guy wore button-down shirts and slacks.

When Rill paused at the door, she glanced over her shoulder at him. He was scanning the wide parking lot. She appreciated the concern, but it did nothing to settle her nerves. The Biltmore had a long street approaching it. How would Bill know if something looked suspicious?

The cool, air-conditioned air hit Ahri, and she shivered. While Rafe checked them in, she scanned the lobby, her gaze settling on a colorful backlit panel of stained glass. She went up to it and read the plaque.

"Designed by Frank Lloyd Wright," Bill said.

"Yeah." The whole place wore a feel of opulence without being vulgar. She hated to admit it, but it impressed her.

They strolled to where Rafe was finishing up. She glanced at the luggage near an elderly couple who were also checking in. Ahri tried to remember what she'd stuffed in her bags. It wasn't like she'd been planning to stay in a hotel tonight.

Rafe turned and handed them each their access keys. "We're in a suite." He headed toward the elevator.

"Have you stayed here before?" she asked, following him inside.

"Once, though it was winter so the weather wasn't too hot."

"You get used to it. Kayn said the hardest thing about attending Harvard was Massachusetts' humidity after having lived here so many years."

"He complained about it all the time," Rafe said with a chuckle, checking out the room numbers as they went down the hall. "Now he likes to complain about the same thing in Boone. That and the snow in the winter."

"I thought he was just kidding. You really have snow in North Carolina?" Ahri asked.

"Our elevation is over 3,000 feet. I think we probably average maybe three feet each winter."

Ahri had never lived anywhere with snow. She wondered if she'd still be there in the winter.

Rafe stopped at a door and unlocked it. She followed him inside, and her jaw dropped. He'd called it a suite, but it looked like an apartment. To the right and left were doors but straight ahead was a little living room with a couch and a couple of chairs. It even had a small kitchen and a dining table with six chairs.

"Wow," she said.

"I understand your feelings," Rafe said from beside her. "The first time I ever stayed in one of these was before our first game went viral."

"You haven't always been rich?" She glanced up at him.

"No. I was a scholarship boy. My mother worked two jobs to make sure I had the right credentials to get into Harvard."

Ahri's admiration for Rafe hitched up even more, and she felt an unexpected sense of connection with him. He'd grown up poor too. Why hadn't her brother ever mentioned that to her?

"Where's Bill going to sleep?" she asked.

"He and I will share that room. There are two beds in there." Rafe pointed to one of the doors as he sat on a couch. He opened his laptop.

"It's really nice of you to put me up in a hotel overnight, but I feel kind of—"

"Don't worry about it." Rafe interrupted with a raised a hand as though to cut off anymore argument about it. "I turned it into a business trip, so it's a tax write-off, and I'd have gotten a suite anyway."

"I'd like to ask Mrs. Meisner some questions before I walk around the hotel," Bill said. "You mentioned that you recognized a man today as the one who followed you. What did he look like?"

"A middle-aged Hispanic man, pretty commonplace around here. If I hadn't been so spooked by what Zed told me, I might not have noticed him."

"Anything else descriptive?"

"He looked fitter than I'd have expected for a man his age." She shivered at the memory of when she'd realized the guy who'd been standing near the corner of her apartment complex had also been outside her office. "He was buff."

"Really buff?" Bill was writing in a notebook.

"Buff enough I could tell. You know how, even if a guy is wearing a dress shirt, it's still obvious that he lifts weights a lot? He looked like that. Besides that, the only other thing that caught my attention was his dangling earring—just one—like a pirate."

"Was it a hoop?" Bill asked.

"No. It looked like a dragon. Or maybe a scorpion. That would have fit his appearance better." Ahri rubbed her forearms, unwilling to explain how that earring and the way the guy'd watched her had freaked her out. Her emotions were too close to the edge, and she didn't want to cry in front of them.

"Interesting." The security man stared off in the distance and nodded before jotting down something else. He stood. "I'm going to check on some things."

"Just order whatever you want from room service," Rafe said to Ahri, looking up from his laptop.

"Yes, order in." Bill glanced at her. "I don't recommend you go to the restaurant for dinner, in case someone followed us here."

"Are you going to work here tonight?" she asked Rafe.

"No. I'm visiting a place we're partnering with." Rafe turned his laptop so she could see the browser he'd opened. "It's called The Gaming Den."

"What's that?

"A place for gamers to gather. It used to be one of those dollar theaters that closed. Our partner had the idea to convert it into rooms where people who play REKD can meet in person and compete on the big screen. It's been surprisingly successful. One of our professional teams even moved to Phoenix so they could use one of the rooms."

"I love the idea." Ahri thought of the LAN parties her brother'd had when they were growing up, where his friends had brought over their computers so they could connect them via a router to play together.

"The owner recently converted one room for virtual reality. And where the old theater had video game machines, they have tables for people who want to play things like *Dungeons and Dragons* or *Magic*, and there's room for board games."

"Did they keep the concessions?"

"That's where he's really making his money. Just like movie theaters."

"Can I come with you?" she asked.

"You *want* to come?" Rafe asked, surprised.

"Oh, please." Ahri rolled her eyes. "Do you really think I could grow up with Kayn and not be a gamer?"

Rafe seemed to think about it, his brows pinched. "Bill, I wasn't planning to bring you along. Can we sneak her out?"

The older man studied her for a second before nodding. "Let me see what I can do."

"You don't usually travel with a bodyguard?" she asked.

"Not normally." Rafe pointed to the left. "That should be your room over there. Why don't you get settled and check out what they're offering for room service?" He turned his laptop back toward him.

Ahri knew when she'd been dismissed, so she went to her room. It probably should have irritated her, but she found it oddly comforting instead. It was like she had Kayn there after all since he had the same focus on work.

She glanced around the room, feeling a little lost. Knowing that Bill and Rafe were out there made her feel more secure than she had since Zed's freaky warning. The worry hadn't left though. She hated not knowing what was going on, what her future would be.

Ahri checked out the toiletries in the bathroom, glad to see they provided what she'd need. Thinking about that night's activities, she smiled for the first time since the whole nightmare had started. The idea of losing herself in a good game fight made her feel better. It might distract her from thinking about Zed.

Could he have gotten involved in gambling? If he owed money to a bookie, would she be obligated to pay it back? She didn't know what Arizona's gambling laws were. Could someone he owed a gambling debt to legally sue her for payment? Or would it be the creepy kind of Mafia Vinnie and Luigi stereotype villain who came after her—*pay up or I'll break your leg*? That one seemed more likely considering her ransacked apartment.

She and Zed had some savings for a down payment on a house that she could use if she needed to. It made her sick to think of using their hard-earned money to pay for something so useless as a gambling debt. Assuming Zed hadn't emptied the account.

Worried, she pulled out her phone and checked the balance. He hadn't touched any of it. None. Her stomach in a knot, Ahri stared at the screen until it went dark on its own. He'd left, and she had no idea where to. As awful as the last year had been with him, she'd cared about him once. She felt helpless, but he'd made it so she couldn't do anything for him.

Ahri picked up the room service menu. Any other time, it all would have sounded good, but nothing appealed to her. It wasn't what she was craving. She took it with her to the living room.

"I've made arrangements for a new car to be delivered," Bill was saying. "It'll be innocuous. I also picked up a hat for Mrs. Meisner since I didn't notice any in her boxes."

"Wait. How would *you* know what I had in my boxes?" She pressed her fingers against the tight muscles in her jaw. Hadn't her privacy already been intruded on enough?

"You're very efficient and wrote the contents on the outside of them," Bill said. "I didn't open anything."

"Oh." Ahri felt stupid. She needed to stop being so prickly. "Okay."

Bill shot Rafe an expectant glance, who nodded. Her stomach knotted even worse. They needed to stop doing that.

"Until we know what's going on," the security man said, "I've counseled your brother to divert your possessions to another state." He explained his concerns. "It might be nothing."

"Or it might be something. I guess it doesn't matter where my things are since I'll be staying with Kayn for a while." She really didn't want to think about it. "Why did you get me a hat?"

"Because you weren't wearing one when we arrived. Hats make people look different. It's an easy disguise in case someone's watching for you." He handed her an

Arizona Diamondback cap. "I recommend you put your hair in a ponytail and pull it up inside when we go out."

"Thank you." Ahri accepted it, filled with a confusion of emotions. "Sorry I've been such a snot today. I appreciate that you two believe me, but, to be honest, it's kind of freaking me out again, like it makes it more real."

"Remember, it's Bill's job to consider possible threats," Rafe looked at her sympathetically. "That's what I pay him the big bucks for."

"Yeah." She played with the hat. How serious was it? Serious enough that someone had searched her apartment. She wasn't normally the kind of person to push off facing hard things, but she was just done tonight. That was when she realized she hadn't called her brother yet.

"I should probably let Kayn know I won't be there tonight."

"He'll be glad to hear from you, but he already knows we won't be back until tomorrow."

"Oh." She handed the menu binder to Rafe. "You sure you want to order room service, or do you want to stop for fast food on the way to your gaming den?"

"You prefer fast food to *this*?" he asked, flipping through it.

"Call it comfort food." She shrugged. "Don't you eat fast food anymore, or are you too much of a big shot for it?"

Rafe sent her a flat look. "My mother runs a bed-and-breakfast. She's probably one of the best cooks in the world. You should hear her rant about the 'slop' they serve at fast food restaurants."

"Rafe is a killer cook himself." Bill grinned at his boss.

"I think I remember Kayn saying something about that, years ago." Ahri smiled and turned her attention to Rafe, curious.

"Oh?" he asked.

"He said he'd have just ordered pizza when you all worked together, but you always insisted on whipping something up. He said he'd have been ticked if you weren't such a good cook."

"I do make a mean pizza," Rafe said with a chuckle.

"While you decide where we're going to eat," Bill said, rising from the couch, "I'd like to ask Mrs. Meisner some more questions."

"Just call me Ahri, please." Her muscles had tensed, and she stretched to ease them.

"All right, Ahri, think back on what your husband said when he left." Bill pulled out his notebook again. "Can you remember the exact words he used? I'm especially interested in how he phrased it."

"Zed said it wasn't safe and asked if I could go to my mother's." Ahri started to pace. "He mentioned a couple of times that it wasn't safe, that people were after him. For nearly a year his work's been really busy with him assigned more accounts. He said he had to work evenings to stay caught up. I commented about it to his secretary once, and she didn't know what I was talking about. He was really stressed when I asked him about it, and he blew up."

"Is this why you were thinking of leaving him?" Rafe asked, his voice soft.

"Six months ago, I wondered if he was having an affair. I reviewed all the transactions in our joint account. I even went through his phone." Ahri flushed at the memory. "I didn't find anything. I kept trying to get him to talk with me, to share, but nothing I did worked. It only made him mad."

"Did he ever hit you?" Bill asked.

"No. I'd have left him for sure if he'd pulled that." One thing Ahri had learned from watching her mother was never to put up with that kind of treatment. "For a few days before he left, he was super stressed. He said he was working late, for the extra money. I called his office yesterday morning, and they said he quit last week."

The memory of her mortification knotted her stomach. How could he have emotionally divorced her so thoroughly and she not realized it? She rubbed the heel of her palm against the pain in her chest. So many secrets. So many lies.

Rafe reached over and covered her other hand between his. She met his gaze, his brown eyes full of compassion and not judgment. He didn't say anything, but for some reason the warmth of his touch calmed her.

"What kind of accounts did he have?" Bill asked.

"He was a CPA for a bank. It was a good job and paid a decent wage. I have no idea what he was doing during the day or into the night for a week. He told me he had meetings." Ahri sighed. "I feel so stupid. He probably wasn't even lying to me, just going to a *different* kind of meeting."

"I'll do some research while we're at the gaming den," Bill said. "I'm curious to see if that scorpion is associated with any gangs or other groups. It could just be some middle-aged man wanting to be cool again."

Ahri wished she could believe that. She wasn't up to date on current events like she should be. The news outlets just focused on all the ugly stuff. She'd had enough of that in her real life, so she'd avoided depressing news. Some people she knew thought that watching other people going through bad situations made their own seem not so awful, but she'd never felt that way. It just brought her down more.

"You okay to order some dinner or do you really want to go out for fast food?" Rafe asked.

She realized then that his hand was still over hers, and it wasn't cold anymore. It made her feel comforted. For the first time, she was glad her brother had sent Rafe instead. Kayn would have been ranting and raving about getting justice for her. She didn't need that right now.

Rafe had always been kind to her when she'd come to Harvard for a visit. They'd talked a lot. One time she'd even thought he might be interested in her, but she'd decided she'd imagined it. Not that it mattered. The next time she came, she was engaged to Zed, and not long after, she'd heard Rafe had a girlfriend.

"Do they serve hot dogs at your gaming den?" she asked.

"Yes." He squeezed her hand and let it go. "Comfort food works just fine for me."

"Well, if you don't mind," Bill said, "I'd rather have a steak. I'll stop at the restaurant when I do my rounds."

"If we have time, I'm going to take a soak." Ahri stood.

"Good plan." Rafe had his laptop open and was already typing away. "I'll get some work done."

Ahri glanced over her shoulder at him as she went to her room. Was work all he did? He needed to have a life outside of this business the four friends had created. She wondered what it would have been like to have met him earlier, before she'd gotten serious with Zed.

She shook off the thought. Fatigue was making her loopy. A bubble bath would be just the answer.

Rafe changed into jeans and a REKD T-shirt before going back into the living room to get in a little more work. He'd finished going through his messages. He might have time to work on some lore for a new champion.

He settled on the couch again and opened his laptop. One of the things the four of them had agreed on when they'd started their business was that they didn't want to be one of those game publishers who created a game and then moved on. Those companies didn't update their games to keep them fresh for the players. It was like finding a program you loved but the company stopped supporting it.

Rafe had been the only one who'd seen the potential to enter the world of Esports, so he'd made sure to keep that as their end goal—and their spring competitions had been even more successful than he'd hoped, with their highest worldwide viewing approaching a quarter of a million people just for the North American teams.

He opened his champion document. They had a team of designers who brainstormed ideas for creating new champions or updating existing ones. Rafe didn't have time to sit in on many of those meetings, but he insisted on keeping his finger in that aspect of the creation.

They'd built the business's structure to encourage creativity from all levels. To succeed with an ongoing game that wasn't a single release, it had to be ever growing and changing. He chuckled softly, remembering the expression on the attorney's face that he was interviewing when he'd told her she would be required to play the game. Everyone was.

From the feedback they'd received, people who played REKD liked the variety of champions, and the difference in skills required to play them, from simple to complex. Some required precise skill shots in battle while others were much simpler. The competitive nature spanned a broad range of interests.

None of the four founders could play the game as well as the pro teams, but it was fun to get invited to one of their skirmishes and test out his own skills. The day when parents used to tell their children they could never make a living playing video games was a thing of the past, not when their pool for the winning MSC team was approaching $2 million. And the prize for the Midsummer Clash would be half that of the World finals.

Rafe felt satisfaction at having helped to create something that garnered so much passion from its players. He loved reading about parents playing with their kids and connecting through their shared love of the game. His game. His and the guys. The lore pages he wrote got as many views as the ones for weapons did, so it was clear that players enjoyed finding out the history of their favorite champions. Someday he might even find somebody he trusted, who could be the CEO instead of him, so he'd be free to play and create like the other guys.

He heard Ahri's door open and glanced over his shoulder. Her cheeks were flushed from her hot bath. She'd pulled her hair back into a ponytail, as Bill had instructed. She wore capris and a colorful blouse, looking very different from when they'd arrived. He found himself staring at her a little too long and turned back to his laptop.

"Bill's not back yet," he said. "If you're hungry, help yourself to the snacks over there."

"I'm fine." She came to stand behind him and leaned over to read what he was writing. "What's this?"

Rafe rubbed the back of his neck, resisting the impulse to close the laptop. He usually didn't let people read the first draft of the stories he wove about the characters. But with everything that Ahri had been through, he was glad to provide something that could distract her from it, even for a little while.

"It's the background for a new champ I'm proposing."

"Intriguing." She came around the couch, sat close beside him, and continued to read.

"This is just the first draft." Rafe fiddled with the laptop cord.

"It's good." She glanced up at him. "Is she going to be human?"

"I haven't decided yet."

"If she is, make her a different race. Your champion pool isn't very balanced."

"What do you mean?'"

"Well, you have lots of nonhumans. Of the humans, you don't have many who are people of color. You only have a few Asians and none are women. There's only a couple of black champions—both guys, by the way—but no Latinos at all. Seriously, you guys need to fix that."

"We've had this discussion before, and we're working on it," Rafe said. "It takes time."

"While you're at it, can you put more armor on your female champions?" Ahri leaned back. "No woman in her right mind would go into battle wearing practically nothing."

"You sound like my mother," Rafe said. "It helps to draw our players to the game, and most of them are guys." He looked down at her. "And several of the male champions wear things like kilts and are bare chested."

"That's a lame excuse."

"I get it, but girl gamers don't go for competitive games like REKD nearly as much as guys do. The motivations are different."

Ahri crossed her arms, and Rafe's face went warm. He wasn't used to being challenged, but he liked her spunk. He and the guys had to work hard to keep their employees from kowtowing to them.

"I get it," he said, "but you were raised with a gamer brother who shared his love of these kinds of games with you. The stats show that female players tend to look for completion rather than competition in their video games."

"Maybe. I think there are probably more female REKD players than will publicly admit it because of the way the guys act when they find out someone on their team is a girl. That's why we choose names that don't identify gender."

"We do periodic surveys of our players," Rafe offered. "I'll make sure they ask that question next time."

"Be sure to ask if girl gamers don't like the clothing choices of female champs."

Rafe was reminded again of Kayn. He had the same dogged determination that his sister did.

"You should talk with Darius about it," he said. "It's his team."

"That's right. Take the lazy way and pass the buck to another founder. You four worked together to create this, so you've all had input." Her disgusted tone now carried a hint of humor, and she didn't quite roll her eyes at him as she shifted to look at him. "REKD is so different from that first game you sold for all that money. Why'd you guys decide to do an online battle arena rather than an app?"

"It was sheer luck that we hit on a hungry market for that first one. The odds of us being able to duplicate it were slim. None of us wanted to retire in our mid-twenties. When Kayn suggested a competitive game, we all liked the idea. I'm the one who thought it had Esports potential. We had the money, so why not?"

"Your MBA probably didn't hurt." Ahri sounded approving now, and Rafe's neck muscles relaxed.

"Well, we needed someone who understood business, and I had my Harvard connections in the field, so here I am." Rafe heaved out a breath.

"Don't you like it?" Ahri asked.

"I don't mind it. I also have a brother-in-law with family connections who were willing to invest. They expected me to be at the helm, so I am. What I love is *this*." Rafe pointed to his laptop.

Ahri watched him for a second, considering, the corner of her mouth curving up. "What do you—"

The door opened, and they both turned.

"You two ready to go?" Bill asked.

"We sure are." Rafe stood and reached out a hand to pull Ahri to her feet.

"Let me get my hat," she said.

"Hang on." Bill held up a package that had a flip-phone in it. "I picked up a burner phone for you in case whoever's after your husband is sophisticated enough to track you that way. Once again, it's a precaution. You should write down only important phone numbers, like your mother's, because I'm taking your phone offline."

"What about my bank account? I checked it tonight."

"Write down those numbers, and then I'll remove the battery."

Chapter 4

A hri was quiet on the drive to the gaming den. For some reason, the phone thing had hit her harder than anything else. She'd been in a dream-like state, but the issue of her electronic footprint being traceable had made it real. Bill seemed committed to making her go silent. While she appreciated that he was trying to keep her safe, it worried her that she might not have access to her money.

The car pulled up to the theater, and she surveyed a giant sign that hung where the marquee would have been with the words *The Gaming Den*, cleverly made up of controllers and board game pieces. They got in line to pay their entrance fee which Rafe handled. She liked that he didn't assume he should get in free.

"I can pay for myself." Ahri did have some cash on her.

"I've got it." Rafe gently touched her arm when she started to argue. "I'm actually looking forward to this as more than a work visit. Please, let me pay for you."

Warmth crept up her face and spread through her body. His dark brown eyes held hers for a second. Then a small crease appeared between them. He blinked and dropped his hand.

"Okay," Ahri said when she could finally get a breath. "Thanks."

All the garbage she'd been dealing with lately must have taken its toll on her. What an emotional mess she was, responding to him like that. She gave herself a mental shake. It was stupid.

When they entered, the smell of popcorn hit Ahri, and her stomach growled. Not wanting to think about whatever that had been with Rafe, she turned her attention to the line of people at the concessions.

On the other side of the lobby was the nook Rafe had mentioned, where two tables had been set up. One had people playing a card game. Based on how they were dressed, one wearing elf ears and another in a mage's robes, she guessed it might be *Magic*.

"What does it cost in utilities for a place this size?" she asked. "Can they make enough at the door and with concessions to pay the overhead?"

"That's the question of the year," Rafe said. "They only opened six months ago. We're trusting that enough gamers want the shared in-person experience. They're advertising at local theaters and online. The numbers have been steadily increasing as word gets out."

Ahri's stomach growled again.

"Sounds like you're ready for dinner," Rafe said with a chuckle.

"Some things I just can't hide." She followed him to the concessions line, glancing back at Bill.

He held back, watching people. Bill had a way about him, meeting people's eyes and nodding his head in acknowledgment, that made him look like a people watcher. He was good at not looking creepy doing it.

"Hot dog, right?" Rafe asked.

"Yes, please. And I really need some chocolate." She moved past him to the rack with the large candy boxes and muttered to herself, "It's been one of those weeks."

"I think you're holding up really well," Rafe said from behind her.

Ahri jumped and put her hand to her heart. "I thought you were getting the dogs."

He held up two long boxes. "I didn't mean to startle you."

"It's okay. Maybe I won't be so jumpy when we're out of Phoenix."

Rafe put the hot dogs on the counter and reached for her box of candy. Pinching her lips, she handed it over.

"Let's eat first." Rafe nodded at some round tables near the concessions counter and strode to a table.

She picked up packets of condiments on the way to join him, watching the people with interest. A group of five guys came from the hallway of theater rooms, all chatting enthusiastically.

Rafe grinned and nodded in their direction. "Listen to them."

Ahri did, and the lingo sounded familiar. "They just finished a game of REKD."

He nodded. "And they won."

The group went to the concessions counter and picked out food, discussing strategies and reliving good plays. Another group of five followed, not looking as happy. She decided they'd lost the match.

"I wish I could lose myself in this world." Ahri took a bite of her hot dog.

"What do you mean?" Rafe sipped from his cup. "Do you want to get a job in a place like this?"

"No," she said when she'd swallowed. "What would I do here? I'm an office manager. I think the innovation part of what you guys are doing is what appeals to me. I'd love to be part of creating something." She shook her head. "I don't know how to explain it. I guess I'm just tired of my life."

"I can understand that. I've felt the same way many times."

"Really?" Ahri studied him. She'd thought he had everything. Not many guys were billionaires before they were thirty.

"I got everything I wanted." Rafe heaved out a breath.

Ahri's heart twisted a little at his obvious unhappiness. No, it wasn't that. Dissatisfaction maybe. Did the other guys know? Kayn had said several times that it was because Rafe was good at what he did that they'd done so well, that he had business savvy. How hard was it for him to be forced into a role just because he was good at it?

Rafe finished his food, lost in his own thoughts. Ahri wondered how old he was. If she remembered right, he was the youngest of the four guys.

"Everything happened so fast," he finally said. "I'd just started the second semester of my graduate program when we got the first offer to sell."

Ahri remembered how excited Kayn had been. The idea of her brother being a millionaire had blown both of them away.

"You talked them into holding out," she said.

"I figured we were doing just fine as we were." Rafe rose and gathered the trash.

"Did you think they'd counter the offer?"

"I didn't." He stood a little taller, and the corner of his mouth twitched. "That was a happy surprise. They *really* wanted the rights to that first game."

"Are you sorry now you sold?" she asked.

"Why do you ask?" Rafe watched her, suddenly wary.

"Because you don't sound happy." Ahri knew that look. She'd seen it in her mirror for months.

"I'm twenty-five and a billionaire. Why shouldn't I be happy?" Rafe gave a stiff shrug and wouldn't look at her. "Ready to check out this place?"

"Sure." Ahri followed him. He acted a lot older than twenty-five. She doubted getting lucky with a game had made him so serious and mature. What had happened in his past to have done that to him? It struck her that he seemed like people she knew who were missing something in their lives. Like herself. It was obvious money couldn't buy everything.

Her thoughts drifted to her brother. Lately, they'd only been able to talk once a week rather than every couple of days. Some of that had been because of the project he was working on, the same one that'd made it hard for him to get away to come for her. Was he unhappy too?

Rafe nodded toward the entrance that led to the hallway of theater rooms. He guided her with a hand on the small of her back.

For some reason Rafe kept his hand there as they walked. She liked the comforting feel of it, the sense of belonging somewhere. His closeness and gentle touch made her feel watched over, protected. It also confused her, and she didn't want to be even more confused right now.

Rafe opened the first door that had sound coming from it. They walked up the ramp. The large theater screen had the loading page for a game of REKD.

"Wow," she breathed. "It's amazing on the big screen. How do they get the game to show at that quality?"

"No idea. The tekkies handle that." Rafe guided her the rest of the way into the room and paused. Bill ducked in behind them.

The seating in the lower three-quarters of the room had the same stadium seating as a theater, probably left over from its former use. A few people sat in the seats, apparently spectators waiting for the game to begin. The big difference came at the top. A platform had been constructed for the two teams of five each. They sat on opposite sides with a large space between them. Like in the professional games, they wore headsets so they could talk to team members.

"I'd like to sit right below one of the teams so I can hear their game chatter," she said.

"Lead the way."

Ahri checked the screen and recognized some of the names. She gasped and glanced back at Rafe. "This is the pro team."

He grinned and nodded. "Do you follow them online?"

"I don't miss a match if I can help it. Forget baseball or soccer. They're boring."

Rafe chuckled and indicated they should move further down the row.

"How much do you play?" he asked as they took their seats.

"Daily, if I can. I guess you could call it my hobby."

The pregame champion bans and selections were finished, and the game started.

"Is this just a practice game?" she whispered, leaning close to Rafe.

"Yes." His warm breath tickled her ear and sent a little tingle down her spine. He smelled really good. She shook her head at the random thought and tried to pull back her thoughts. He added, "The Midsummer Clash will be held in Miami."

"Will you be broadcasting it in any of the rooms here?" Ahri asked. "I think it'd be a fun shared experience."

"We've talked about it. The owner ought to make a killing on concessions."

"Enough to make this month's rent anyway," Ahri said.

"Let's hope so. If enough people enjoy coming, this could turn into a lucrative investment."

"You already get huge crowds at the live locations," she said. "I'll bet there are plenty of people who'd like to watch the events together, but they'd need to know about them. Theaters broadcast special events like plays. Imagine if locals could win tickets to come here to watch a live broadcast of the Clash finals. It might be good advertising."

Rafe gave a soft grunt like he was thinking about it and turned his attention to the game. As usual, Ahri found herself wrapped up in the game play. She loved to watch how the pro players used clever spell or attack combinations when they used her favorite champion's wombo-combos. It was a close game. When it ended and the pro team won, she jumped to her feet with the others, applauding.

At the end, the lights brightened, and a man entered.

"That's Tim Nasus, the owner." Rafe stood.

"I just heard you'd sneaked in. Everyone," the man pointed to Rafe, "we have a special guest tonight. This is Rafe Davis, one of the creators of REKD."

Everyone gathered around them, and Ahri stepped back. Bill was at her side in an instant, keeping an eye on the small crowd. Rafe did a good job of answering questions. Finally, he looked back at her.

"We've been invited to play. Are you interested?"

"I'm only Ruby 5, so I'm not that highly ranked," she said.

"It's just in fun," Rafe said.

"I'll play," she said, glancing at the pro team members, "but go easy on us, okay?"

"No way." Rafe frowned. "If we win, I don't want anyone to say they threw the game for us."

"Fine. I call support." Ahri glanced at the team stations. "Where do I sit?"

She was surprised when Bill took up one of the seats. He took the jungle role which seemed to suit him. The five-member team was filled out by two people from the audience.

Ahri had never played with Rafe before. He was really good. One of the things she loved about the support role was watching out for her team members. In the game it was easy for her to forget her problems and do something she could control. She and Rafe partnered well on the bottom battle lane. Their team put up a good fight, but in the end, they were spanked.

"That was fun." She shook everyone's hands, surprised to find how much more relaxed she was.

Rafe talked with Mr. Nasus for a few minutes while the players queued up for another game.

"Do you have to stand around being bored stupid very often?" she asked Bill.

"It's never boring to watch a game." Bill nodded toward Rafe who was approaching them.

"You ready to go?" he asked.

"If you are," she said. "Thanks for letting me come."

Rafe took his seat beside Ahri, surprised at how much he'd enjoyed the evening. She looked better than she had when they'd left the hotel, so it'd been a good break for her. He was glad.

With Kayn so busy the next couple of weeks, Rafe wondered if Ahri would receive the kind of support she'd need. The idea that she'd be better off at his mother's bed-and-breakfast kept coming to mind. With two young children and a garden to help tend, there'd be plenty to keep her distracted.

"It's probably too soon to ask about your plans," Rafe began and immediately wished he hadn't spoken.

"*Plans.* I wish I knew what to do." Ahri looked away from him, out the window. "Leaving my job here with a day's notice has burned that bridge. It might be hard to get another job."

"I meant your plans for Zed."

She turned to face Rafe, and their gazes met. "You mean besides divorce him?"

"I've assumed you'd do that, since it seems the only sensible thing to do. Are you still in love with him?" He groaned. "Sorry. Sometimes my brain rattles around like a BB in a boxcar."

"What?" She stared at him in confusion.

"It's an expression that means I'm stupid. I shouldn't have asked you such a personal question."

"It's okay. I haven't loved him in . . . I don't know. A long time. He's not the man I married." She made that motion again, rubbing her chest, like her heart hurt. "I just don't understand where we went wrong. I think that hurts the most. I feel like such a failure."

"I get it." Rafe wasn't about to go into his own relationship issues. "Just know that you have whatever time you need. Not just from Kayn. I'll support you in whatever you need. And the other guys will too."

"Thank you." Ahri glanced at him, her eyes glistening.

Rafe wished he could do more for her.

K ayn was waiting at the airport when they landed. Rafe watched as Ahri ran from the plane and leaped into her brother's arms. He glanced at Rafe and mouthed *thank you* before grabbing the handle of her large suitcase. She carried the glass carrier for her mother's doll, and they went to his car, both talking at once.

"I've got my team working on this," Bill said, stepping beside him. "How deeply do you want us to dig?"

"As deep as you have to." Rafe rubbed at the tight muscles in his neck. "If it's really ugly, we may want to let Kayn break it to her."

"You don't think it's going to end well." It wasn't a question.

"No, I don't."

"I think she's stronger than you're giving her credit for." Bill clapped Rafe on the back. "And I think she may be angry if she finds out you've kept information from her."

"That's why I'll leave it up to Kayn." Rafe didn't know what to think—or feel—about Ahri Meisner. She was already taking up way too much of his brain capacity at the moment. He had work to do, and he didn't need the distraction.

"Well, I'm going to take my wife to dinner. I'll see you tomorrow."

"Thanks, Bill."

Rafe glanced after Ahri one last time before heading to the car waiting for him.

After an afternoon spent in meetings where Rafe's mind was distracted by thoughts of Ahri, he was glad to leave work behind and drive to his mother's house. His shoulders relaxed as the blossoming trees sped past. His favorite seasons were spring and fall.

The old bed-and-breakfast had belonged to his grandmother, who'd left it to his mother. His wheelchair-bound father was supposed to have helped run it, but all he'd managed to do was to complain about everything, especially about his "loser" wife and son.

Rafe took a deep breath to calm himself. Thoughts of his father never failed to rile him. For years his mother had tried to convince Rafe that his father used to be a different man, that two car accidents, one including a serious head injury, had changed the man's personality. A selfish, verbally abusive man was all Rafe remembered. He would never understand why his mother had stayed with him if he'd turned into such a different person than the man she'd married. For Rafe, his father being trapped in a wheelchair had never been reason enough for her to stay.

An image of Ahri talking about Zed last night floated into Rafe's mind. She hadn't flinched one bit when she'd said she was going to divorce her husband. She was a feisty one. If things had been bad between them for a year, Rafe was surprised she'd stayed so long. Maybe she was more like his mother than he was giving Ahri credit for. The B&B might be just the place for her to pull her life together.

"Rafe! Rafe!" His five-year-old sister Lessa came running down the wide porch steps as he drove up to the house. He hit his brakes and shot her a disapproving frown. She pulled to a stop, looking appropriately abashed.

"You know better than to come running at a moving car like that," he said out his open window. "What would Ma say if she'd seen you?"

"I *did* see her." His mother scooped up the child, gave her a quick hug, and then a stern look.

"Sorry, Ma." Lessa's bottom lip trembled like she was going to cry.

"Go tell your daddy that Rafe is here." Francie set her down, and the little girl ran back up the steps.

"Hey, Ma." Rafe pulled her into a hug, loving how she smelled—like the fresh outdoors and delicious food coming out of the oven.

"Let me look at you." She pulled back and searched his face. "That job is making you old."

"What? Do I have gray hair?" He bent to search his reflection in his side mirror, fighting back a smile.

"Oh, stop teasing me." Francie slid her arm through his, and they headed toward the house. "Please tell me you're dating someone. You need to have a life, you know."

"REKD Gaming *is* my life right now." And the company wouldn't desert him.

"Honey, it shouldn't be. Are you going to turn into a young Boomer, married only to your job?"

Rafe's thoughts flashed to Ahri. Startled and confused at the mental leap, he didn't know what to say, so he changed the subject.

"How's the garden coming?" he asked.

She heaved out a big breath but didn't push it. That was one of the things he'd always loved about his mother. She might nag him, but she knew not to push things too far.

"The garden is coming along well enough," Francie said. "Another couple of weeks of hard work, and it'll all be in. Alex has finals this week, so he's not able to help much, but I'll be okay."

One of the things Rafe liked about his college professor stepfather was how much he loved working on this house with Francie. Before Rafe had gone to college, he and she had always done the garden together. Now that he was back in Boone, REKD consumed most of his time. Once the launch was completed, he could spend more time helping. He wondered if Ahri had ever gardened. There he went again, thinking of her.

"We have company staying at the complex," he said.

"Anyone I know?"

They stepped inside, and Rafe closed his eyes and took a deep breath, enjoying the familiar and delicious smell of one of his mother's savory casseroles. The scent had a bit of tang to it, so he guessed she'd added jalapenos. He opened his eyes and found his mother watching him expectantly.

"What can I say?" He gave her his best cheeky grin. "I love your cooking."

Francie shook her head, but her cheeks had flushed at the compliment. He didn't think she'd ever get used to people complimenting her. That was what came from so many years living with his father, who couldn't see the good in anything. Or anyone. At least Alex had helped her to believe that what people said about her cooking was true.

They entered the kitchen. The large room's modern look still gave him pause. When his mother and stepfather had married, Alex had sold his condo and used the money to make improvements on the house. They'd done a lot to the kitchen. The only thing left from his childhood was the large, worn wooden table that served as Francie's work station and where the family ate when they didn't have company.

"Do you have guests tonight?" Rafe asked.

"They're eating out. It's just us." Francie nodded to a stack of plates and went back to mixing the salad. "Well, are you going to tell me who's staying with you or leave me hanging?"

"Sorry." He picked up the plates. "It's Kayn's sister."

"Ah. The Korean beauty with the unexpected green eyes." Francie opened the oven and removed a large casserole dish, the spicy smell making his mouth water. "Is she on vacation?" She shot him a sidelong glance. "Is her husband with her this time?"

Rafe debated internally how much he should share. He didn't want to intrude on Ahri's privacy, but if he was going to suggest she stay here, his mother needed to know part of the story.

"Her husband left her, and in a bad situation. We don't know what he was involved with, but her life's a mess right now."

"That poor thing." His mother paused in tossing the salad, thoughtful. "And y'all are so busy right now. If there's anything I can do for her, let me know. I'd tell her myself, but then she'd think I was putting my nose in her business."

Her kind heart was another thing he loved about his mother.

"There might be something you could do."

She watched him, waiting.

"As you said, Kayn's really busy right now. He'll do his best by her, but you know how distracted he gets when he's in the middle of a project."

"She needs her mother." Francie carried the salad to the table. "Isn't she still alive?"

"Kayn said she moved back to Korea." Rafe went to the silverware drawer. "She wanted the kids to be American and rarely spoke Korean at home. Kayn's mentioned how uncomfortable it is to look Korean but not speak much of the language. Ahri wouldn't like going to be with her mother."

"You seem to know a lot about her," his mother said with a sly glance.

"I don't know about that. We've chatted a lot when she's visited Kayn, and he's talked about her. Sometimes it seems like I know her better than I really do." Rafe paused, thinking about what he'd just said. "That sounds a little presumptuous of me, doesn't it?"

"No." Francie patted his cheek. "It's because you have a good heart and connect with people. I think that's why you're so good with the stories you tell about your game world. You're creative, meaning you can empathize. I heard somewhere that people who read fiction are better at sympathizing with people than those who don't."

"I didn't know you read the champion lore."

"I started when I found out you were the one writing it."

"And you like it?" He couldn't keep the doubt from his voice.

"Of course I like it."

"Because you're my mother." Rafe straightened a knife on the table.

"Because it's *good.*" Francie waggled a finger at him. "Don't doubt me, or I'll have to cancel your birth certificate."

He chuckled at the familiar threat. "The next couple of weeks are going to be crazy for the guys and their teams. I'm worried that if she stays with Kayn, she's going to be lonely. I think it'd be better for her to be around normal people."

"Well, thank you for saying I'm normal," his mother said as she tested the casserole. "I assume you're thinking it'd be good for her to stay here."

"Yes." Rafe always appreciated how well his mother understood him. Maybe that came from her being so young when she'd had him and the need they'd had to protect each other from his father.

"I'm really busy with the kids and the garden right now. I'd love company if you think she'd be willing to help out."

"Anything that tires her out enough to sleep at night should be good for her."

Francie shot him a shrewd glance, and he wondered what it was about.

"She can stay in our personal guest room if she wants." Francie carried the casserole to the table, and Rafe hurried over with the pot holder for her to set it on. "I could even offer to pay her if you think she'd accept it."

"Ask her. Ahri had a good job she was forced to leave behind."

"I don't understand. Why was she forced to leave her job? Lots of women go through divorces and stay right where they're at."

"This is between you and me," Rafe said, deciding to trust his mother's discretion. "Someone ransacked her apartment the day after her husband took off, and she said someone had been following her."

"Oh, my. And her husband just took off?" His mother's eyes flashed. "What a snake in the grass."

From the living room came the sounds of children squealing and a man's heavy steps. Alex Diederik came into the kitchen with a child clinging to each of his legs.

"I seem to have acquired a couple of growths," he said, and the children giggled.

Rafe watched as his stepfather leaned over to kiss his wife. That was something Rafe had never seen growing up. Francie had been skittish and closed off around Rafe's father. Thanks to Alex's tender care, she was a different person.

"I hope you brought your appetite," she said.

"I'm so hungry my belly thinks my throat's been cut," Alex said.

Rafe's stomach growled, and they laughed. He squatted down. "How about a hug, Lessy-wessy?" She released her father's leg and threw her arms around his neck.

"Me too. Me too." Four-year-old Nik did the same thing, and Rafe rose with them in his arms. Growing up, he'd always wished he'd been part of a larger family. He hadn't expected it to finally happen after he'd left for college.

The children kept the meal lively. When they'd finished dinner and had cleaned up, they gathered in the living room. Lessa approached Rafe and took his hand, her little face serious.

"Can I play you a song on the piano?"

"Please do," Rafe said, and she skipped to the instrument Alex had brought with him from his condo.

The song was short but well played. Rafe asked, "When did she start taking piano lessons?"

"A new neighbor gives lessons after school. Sara Fortune is a teacher at the elementary school," his mother said. "She's a real sweetheart, and Lessa loves her classes. Mrs. Fortune is trying to start a program for kids who can't afford to pay."

"If those kids can't pay for lessons, how can they afford a piano to practice on?" Rafe asked.

"That's part of what she needs help with," Alex said, "besides other teachers. She has access to some electronic keyboards the kids can use."

Rafe's mind went to work considering logistics of what this piano teacher was proposing, and he saw a lot of problems.

"How would the children practice every day?"

"She's talking about them coming to her house for that." Alex looked dubious. "Sounds like it has the potential to turn into a nut house unless she has a lot of help. I wouldn't want to be there while a bunch of little kids were pounding away on keyboards."

"She says she's taught groups before, and they'll wear headsets to practice," Francie said. "She knows how to keep things orderly."

"I'll mention it to Ezreal to see if he might like to help." Rafe's mother looked dubious that time. His partner Ez was a brilliant musician but was incredibly shy around people he didn't know. He stuttered when he was stressed, and he was especially stressed around women. "Look how good he is with Lessa and Nik, not nervous at all."

"Maybe." His mother looked thoughtful. "It might be good for him to get out and do something outside of work."

"She's not in too big a hurry, is she?" Rafe asked as he typed a reminder into his phone. "I won't mention it to him until after the newest update is finished. What's her name again?"

"Sara Fortune," Alex said. "She's divorced with a couple of kids."

Rafe nodded. Ez wasn't put off by his mother, so working with another motherly female type shouldn't be a problem for him.

"I like Mrs. Fortune," Lessa said. "She's nice."

"Yes, she is." Francie stood. "I reckon it's time for you lot to get ready for bed."

"Ma," Rafe said, rising, "do you want me to invite Ahri to stay here, or do you want to do it?"

"I think you should." She picked up Nik, who was starting to look drowsy. "We've met a few times, but I'm not sure she'll even remember who I am. It might seem strange to her. She knows you better."

"All right. I'll let her settle in for a couple of days, maybe through the weekend." Rafe picked up his jacket. "She might be ready for a change by Sunday." For some reason, the image of Ahri working with his mother appealed to him.

Ahri paced the apartment again. Bill had suggested she keep her identity as Kayn's sister a secret, and she was going crazy locked inside. Peeking through his curtains to the complex outside, she felt jealous. Even on a Saturday, the place was busy and everyone seemed to have things to do and places to go. She had nothing to occupy her mind and keep her from worrying.

She'd hardly seen Kayn in the three days since she'd been there. She knew he was busy, but she hadn't imagined just how busy. Everyone seemed so driven. The part of her brother's wing that connected with the main office building included meeting rooms. Sometimes she'd sneak a look out his apartment door and overhear the brainstorming going on in the conference rooms. Something about one of the champion updates wasn't working the way they wanted it, and everyone sounded stressed.

When she'd first seen the drawings for the complex, it hadn't occurred to her just how close her brother's working and living spaces were. Maybe that was part of the reason Kayn couldn't break himself away from the job. It was right *there* on the other side of his apartment door. With each of the four partners having their own wings, she imagined they all had trouble separating their business and personal lives.

Ahri went to the window and stared at the garden beds artistically spread around the grounds. The weather was a lot cooler here than in Phoenix, and the colorful flowers almost cheered her up.

When Kayn had taken her grocery shopping on Saturday, she'd found the town of Boone to be a green delight after living in the desert of Phoenix. The town had fewer than twenty thousand people and felt small-town by comparison. Boone seemed full of young people, mainly students at Appalachian State. The southern accents and fun sayings made her smile when she least expected it.

It surprised Ahri that she felt no pull to return to Arizona. With Zed's leaving and everything that'd happened since, she'd been trying to understand how her life had fallen apart. A couple of her friends had moved out of state, and they'd lost touch. Another friend had married, and her husband and Zed hadn't hit it off. Gradually, they'd drifted apart. Ahri hadn't realized how hard it could be to make "couple" friends. Now that she was alone, she saw how isolated she'd let herself become.

Once this thing with Zed was resolved, what should she do, return to Arizona? With her mother gone, she didn't really have anyone there except for Taliyah. Bill had let Ahri call her but only on one of his phones that had some kind of scrambling software on it. She and Taliyah had talked a couple of times, but it was a little depressing. The office had already moved someone up into Ahri's position.

She studied the people hurrying around and the small groups who were basking in the spring sunshine, most busy talking. They gave off an energy she'd never experienced before in a workplace.

Ahri put on a hoodie and went out Kayn's private entrance at the back of his wing. She hoped the sun would take the edge off the chill. The gardeners must have already finished with his patio area because the flower beds held brightly colored blooms. She walked past the small barbecue and took a seat on a wooden bench. The enclosed area wasn't big enough to host a large gathering, but she could see him having the guys over after work or maybe key members of his programming team for a working dinner.

She liked being close enough to see her brother every day. She'd missed him. He'd assured her that his super busy schedule would settle down in a few weeks. If she stayed here, what should she do? She couldn't just hang around her brother's apartment, nice as it was.

Maybe she could go back to school, but to study what? She'd looked at jobs online, and there were some possibilities. Would any employer hire someone who'd essentially walked off the job, regardless of the circumstances? She'd had a job since she was sixteen. Even these few days off, with nothing to work toward, were driving her a little crazy. She needed to do something.

"Ahri," a familiar man's voice called.

She glanced over her shoulder and found Rafe coming through the short gate.

"Hey," she said, glad to see his bright smile. "I'm surprised you're not in a meeting. I swear you guys have more of them than I've ever seen anywhere I've worked."

"That's the collaborative nature of creative work." He sat beside her on the bench and stretched his legs out in front of him. "How are you doing?"

"Getting a little acquainted with the area." She stared off in the distance. "It's pretty here, so green."

"I asked how *you're* doing."

Ahri looked at him, and her heart did a funny little twitch at the concern on his face.

"I'm still finding my way. Going a little stir crazy."

"Have you heard anything from Zed?"

"How?" She rubbed her hands that had turned cold. "I don't have that phone anymore, remember?" She met Rafe's gaze. "I was worried he might have emptied our savings account. I wouldn't put it past him."

"He hasn't?"

"I had Bill check for me. It was all still there. He didn't even withdraw his half."

"That's odd." Rafe shifted toward her. "Could he be lying low?"

"I guess." Ahri's eyes stung, and she looked away. "He has to be living on something though."

"Did you take out your portion?"

"Yes. Bill helped with that too." Ahri sighed. "I want to get the divorce paperwork going, but how can I serve him if I don't know where he is?"

The decision still made her feel like a quitter, but she felt in her core that it was the right thing to do. She wouldn't be her mother and waste her life hanging onto a man who didn't want her.

"Once again," Rafe said, "Bill's on that. He'll let us know as soon as he has anything."

"Thanks."

Rafe leaned forward and rested his elbows on his knees. "I have a favor to ask you."

"What?" Ahri asked, perking up. Somebody needed her for something?

"You might remember my mother."

"Maybe if I saw her. There's always been so many people at every event I've attended."

"True. She and my stepfather run a bed-and-breakfast." Rafe grinned. "She's the world's most amazing cook ever."

"You said something like that when you picked me up." Ahri remembered Bill's comment at the hotel. "Is that where you learned it?"

"She taught me everything I know, but she's way out of my league." Rafe leaned back again. "She grows most of her own food and has an amazing garden. When I was in high school, I used to help her put it in and maintain it because we couldn't jump over a nickel to save a dime."

"What?" Ahri asked with a laugh.

"Sorry." He gave a soft chuckle. "It means we were poor. We grew most of our own food."

"What about your father?" The flash of anger that crossed his face told her everything. She reached out and touched his hand. "Say no more. I get it."

"I've worked to help support the family since I was sixteen," he said.

"Me too," she whispered.

He met her gaze, and she was struck by the warmth in it. It seemed they had a lot more in common than she'd realized. No wonder he and Kayn got on so well.

"Anyway," Rafe continued, now looking at his hands, "after I went to college, she had to do all the work of putting it in herself. My father died about the time I graduated from high school. Luckily, she remarried a year later, and she and my stepfather turned the old house into a bed-and-breakfast. Her garden's even bigger now, believe it or not. She feeds her guests and even does some catering."

"It sounds like a lot of work." She wondered what all of this had to do with her.

"They also have two young kids."

"Really?" Ahri couldn't imagine her mother having any more children. She was doing so much better now she'd moved back to Korea and had lots of family support there. The thought brought a rush of guilt that Ahri hadn't been able to provide that.

"Lessa's in kindergarten, and Nikolas will start next year. They're not big enough to be much help yet. My stepfather helps where he can, but he's a college professor and this is finals week."

"Are you telling me all this," Ahri asked, understanding what he wasn't saying, "because you want me to help your mother with her garden?"

"Simply put, yes." He heaved out a breath. "I can afford to hire somebody to do it for her, but she won't let me. Believe me, I've tried more than once since I first moved back."

"I like the sound of her. An independent woman. I feel the same way when Kayn tries to fix everything for me with his money." Ahri gave a soft laugh. "Though I confess that I'm glad he was in a financial position to help me move so fast, otherwise I could still be driving here in a moving van."

Rafe just smiled but said nothing else. She decided she liked that about him. The idea of working outside in this beautiful spring weather and creating something that would grow appealed to her. There would also be fewer people than there were here.

"All right. I'll give it a try," Ahri said. "Be warned that I've never done much gardening, but I'm a fast learner."

"Thank you. She said she'd be happy to pay you, but I wonder . . ." His words drifted off, and he shifted in his seat. Was he uncomfortable?

"Wonder what?" she asked, wary.

"Would you like to stay there for a few days?"

"Like *live* there?" When he nodded, she asked, "Why?"

"Because it's a nut house here right now. As long as the creek don't rise, we'll settle down after the release in a couple of weeks."

"Creek don't rise?" Ahri was loving these quaint sayings, especially coming out of this handsome Harvard man who, except for his accent, sounded sophisticated.

If she wasn't careful, she'd pick up that southern drawl too.

"I'm sorry." Rafe tossed up his hands. "The longer I'm back here, the more my youth comes out of my mouth."

"Don't stop on my account. I like it."

"Do you?" He peered at her.

That funny thing happened in her stomach again. Rafe Davis had a way of looking at her in a thrilling but unsettling way. Did he use that in business meetings to cow any dissent? Not with employees, she was pretty sure. If those collaborative brainstorming meetings were any indication of how he ran this business, then it wouldn't be his style.

"I do," she said. "Now tell me more about me staying at your mother's."

"I thought, considering everything you've been through, that it might be good for you to spend some time somewhere normal, in a simple house with home-cooked meals and some good hard work to make you tired enough to sleep at night."

Ahri looked down at her hands. Was it that obvious that she was having trouble sleeping?

"Does she have room if she's running a B&B? I don't want to take away from her income."

"It's a large house, and they keep a private guest room for when they have nonpaying company. Ma says you can stay there."

Ma. He called his mother Ma. It sounded so down-to-earth.

"I thought it'd give you some quiet time, and it'll force Kayn to take a break when he comes to see you." Rafe gave a dark chuckle. "Having our apartments right here in the complex might save commuting time, but it's almost impossible to get away from work. The four of us will be sure to come for dinner at Ma's every Sunday until the launch, and then probably more often after that."

"You think I'll be stuck there for two weeks?" Rafe shot Ahri a look that made her realize how bad that had sounded, and she quickly added, "Not that I'll be *stuck* there. Sorry. That came out wrong. You're saying I can help you and my brother by staying out of your hair and working for your mother for a couple of weeks."

"Yes." His words were simple and direct. "Though I wouldn't call it staying out of our hair. But you don't have to decide now. Just think about it." Rafe rose and looked about to walk away, but she took his hand. He went very still.

"I'll do it. I'm already going a little stir crazy in that apartment. I like the idea of being busy with something useful."

"Great," he said, still not moving. "I'll let Ma know."

"When does she need me?"

"How about I take you when we all go over for dinner on Sunday? You can pack what you need and bring it with you."

"Perfect." She dropped his hand and instantly missed the warmth of his touch. Was that a sign of how lonely she was?

Ahri watched as he walked back toward his wing, rubbing the hand that she'd held. Curious.

Chapter 6

R afe made sure to arrive early to his mother's house on Sunday so he could help with the food prep. The guys had all decided to take their own cars anyway. Ezreal almost hadn't come to dinner because Ahri would be there. Rafe had to assure him that he wouldn't have to talk to her since they'd already been introduced at the ribbon cutting over a year ago.

As they so often did lately, Rafe's thoughts drifted to Ahri. How had a smart girl like her fallen for an idiot like Zed, who hadn't seen what a gift he'd had? Would she end up like her mother in Korea, alone and bitter, never allowing herself a chance at another relationship? Or would Ahri fall into the trap he'd seen too often when girls always went for the same type of jerk? He hoped once she got to know his mother and saw what a loving relationship should look like that Ahri would know there was something better for her.

Rafe gave himself a mental shake. Since when had he become invested in her future happiness? It was none of his business, and she had a brother to watch out for her.

When he drove up to the house, Lessa and Nik waited this time for the car to come to a stop before they ran off the porch. Nik tried the clinging-to-the-leg thing, but Rafe picked him up instead. Lessa took his other hand and skipped while they walked inside, chattering all the time about her day and how much she was looking forward to her next piano lesson. He wondered if that would last very long, or if she'd soon resist the inevitable practicing that friends had griped about. His family had never been able to afford lessons.

"Ma! Rafe is here," Lessa called in a sing-song voice.

"In the kitchen."

Lessa skipped back the way they'd come, probably to wait for the others to arrive. Nik wriggled from Rafe's arms and ran to the corner and some toys he must have been playing with earlier.

Rafe found his mother working at the counter. He kissed her cheek.

"Alex is finishing some work upstairs." She brushed aside a dark curl that had escaped her ponytail. "He's already expanded the table and set it."

"What can I do to help?" Rafe asked.

"I need you to make the dessert," she said. "Put on an apron."

He chose one that didn't have ruffles on it. "What's on the menu?"

"I was going to have you make pecan pie, but I forgot I was out of pecans."

Tying the apron around his waist, Rafe glanced at the counter where she'd put the ingredients and spotted the rolled oats.

"Hillbilly Pie it is." Most of Rafe's happiest childhood memories came from cooking in this kitchen beside his mother. He hadn't understood when he was little that the kitchen had been their refuge from his father. The man hadn't liked the room, maybe because he was afraid someone might ask him to help. Because money had been tight, Rafe and his mother had experimented with recipes. That reminded him that he needed to stock his kitchen at the complex, so he could do some cooking there too. Maybe after the push was over.

They worked in a comfortable silence for a while. It reminded him of what a good team they'd made as he was growing up. She'd been so young when she married, right out of high school. By the time she'd been his age, she'd had a six-year-old son and a disabled husband.

"This is fun," he finally said. "I haven't baked in forever."

"You need to find a hobby, something that doesn't have anything to do with your business. Sometimes you need to give it a break." Francie tapped his nose with her finger. "Listen to your mama. I promise you'll find the time away will make you more productive when you go back to work after."

"'Cuz mama knows best," he quoted.

"Dang right." Alex came into the kitchen, swept his wife into his arms, and kissed her. When he started nuzzling her neck, she squealed.

"Behave yourself." Francie gave him a playful smack on the arm, her cheeks flushed.

Rafe loved to watch how his stepfather treated her. His mother knew Alex treasured her, and it made her shine. Maybe that came from both having been married to such ugly people before.

Having met Alex's sharp-tongued shrew of a first wife a couple of times, Rafe had decided that had been plenty. Victoria was all about money and prestige, the kind of person he'd vowed never to be like. She was so different from his mother.

When Rafe was growing up, Francie had always worked hard to create a loving home, but the "monster in the closet" in the form of his father had always been lurking in the background. The house had such a different feel to it now.

His mother put Alex to work chopping vegetables for a salad, and Rafe turned his attention back to the familiar motions of baking. He *had* been working too hard. His thoughts drifted back to that night at The Gaming Den and how much he'd enjoyed himself. It might have technically been a business trip but having Ahri there had made it fun. He needed to play more.

He was just putting the Hillbilly Pie into the oven when Lessa squealed out on the porch. Someone else had arrived. Rafe washed his hands and removed the apron. He peeked around the corner into the living room. Ezreal had Nik clinging to his leg, while Lessa was talking up a storm. Ez really liked kids. It was too bad he had such a hard time around unfamiliar people. Wearing a silly grin, he let the children guide him to their toys.

"I sure like him," his mother said from beside Rafe. She handed him some linen napkins to fold. "I have Ahri's room all ready for her. I thought she'd come with you."

"Kayn wanted to bring her. I think he feels guilty she's leaving already."

"But it's only for a couple of weeks," Alex said, still chopping.

"That's what she told him." Rafe put another folded napkin in the stack. "I think it's good for them to spend some time together. He's got a solid head that she needs right now."

"You're sure keeping an eye on her. Is she devastated by the breakup?" Francie asked softly.

"Not from what she said." Rafe paused, thinking of his mother's first comment. He *had* been paying extra attention to how Ahri was doing. Was it presumptuous of him to assume he understood her? "Let me rephrase that. Ahri said things hadn't been good between them for a while, and that she'd been thinking of leaving him. The only surprise was that Zed initiated the split."

"I imagine there's bound to be emotional pain there," his mother said. "Recognizing that a relationship is dying isn't quite the same thing as when it actually dies. I'll try to be sensitive. It may do her good to talk, but it may also be better for her to have silence as she works through her feelings."

"You're the best person I know to be her sounding board if she wants one." Alex shot his wife a tender look.

The sound of car engines and tires on gravel announced the arrival of two vehicles. Kayn and Darius must have driven up at the same time. Rafe put the last napkin under a fork. Glancing in the mirror, he checked how he looked. He didn't want to see Ahri again with any flour on his nose.

That was when he spotted his mother watching him in the reflection, her mouth curved in a soft smile. Embarrassed, Rafe straightened his shirt and strode from the kitchen. The guys came to most Sunday dinners, and he didn't usually greet them when they got there, but he wanted to see how Ahri was doing.

Was this pull to her a sign that he was turning into his mother, who had an eye for suffering people? She had a way of offering comfort and understanding. He'd always called it her "mothering instinct." He wasn't sure the title was a good fit for himself.

Ahri stared at the beautiful old home. The green roof made her think of *Anne of Green Gables*. She was already in love with the place. With the green lawns and walkway lined with flowers, it had a welcoming feel to it. The wide porch that surrounded it held an eclectic assortment of rocking chairs that seemed to call to her.

"This way." Kayn pointed to the house and headed to it.

Unlike her brother who left her to follow, Rafe would have guided her with his hand on her back. Ahri pushed away the random thought. She shouldn't be thinking about things like that while she was still married to Zed. She'd done some research. In North Carolina, they had to be separated a year before they could divorce. If she returned to Arizona, she could get one in sixty days, but that was only after he was served. Bill still had nothing on Zed's location.

Ahri paused on the porch and ran a hand over the red fabric of a rocking chair's cushion. The sound of many voices, laughing and talking at once, came from inside. Since everyone knew each other so well, she felt like an outsider.

She sat in the chair and started rocking, inhaling the lovely smell of lilacs. Someone—Rafe's mother, maybe— had put some cut ones in a vase on the little table to the side. This would be a great place to detox from the ugliness that had been her life the last year. Peaceful.

To her left, the screen door opened.

"Not ready to come inside yet?" Rafe asked.

Ahri glanced up at him, expecting pity in his expression but finding understanding instead. She waved at the chair on the other side of the flowers, and he moved to it.

She didn't say anything and neither did he. Rafe Davis was turning out to be a comfortable person to be around.

"You grew up here?" Ahri finally asked.

"Yes. It looks a lot better now. We were barely able to keep the tax collectors away. Ma and Alex have put a lot of money and labor into fixing it up."

"It's lovely."

"Hey, what are you two doing out here?" Kayn opened the screen door. "Aren't you coming inside?"

Rafe stood abruptly, a flash of irritation crossing his face. But it was gone almost as fast as it'd come. "I should probably check on my pie anyway."

"You made a *pie?*" she asked, impressed. "What kind?"

"Hillbilly Pie." At her confusion, he added, "It's pecan pie for po' folks. Ma ran out of nuts."

Ahri gave a soft *hmm* as she rose and followed the guys inside. Maybe Bill hadn't exaggerated when he said Rafe was a good cook. Whatever was for dinner smelled heavenly.

Ezreal sat in a corner playing cars with a little boy. The child must be the baby Rafe's mother had held at the grand opening of the complex. That had been a rushed visit for Ahri because she hadn't had much vacation time.

"You know the guys," Kayn was saying.

Ezreal gave her a nod but didn't meet her gaze. Kayn had warned her the first time she'd been introduced to Ezreal that the man suffered from extreme shyness, so she didn't expect more.

"Nice to meet you again." Darius extended his hand, and she shook it. He'd grown a beard since she'd last seen him. He was the oldest of the four and had been working as an art teacher when they'd created the first game.

"Same here," she said. "How are you liking Boone?"

"It's a nice little place."

"Come meet Rafe's parents." Kayn took her elbow and pulled her away.

"Hello again, Ahri," Rafe's mother said, taking her hands in both of hers.

"Thank you for having me."

"This is my husband, Alex Diederik."

"It's a pleasure." The handsome man with gray at his temples extended a hand.

"I understand you teach at the university." Ahri said, shaking it. "What subjects?"

"History." He put his hand on the head of a dark-haired little girl. "This is Lessa."

The child was scrutinizing her.

"Hello," Ahri said.

"They said Kayn is your brother," Lessa said.

"Yes, he is."

"But he's Korean. How come you got green eyes?"

"Lessa!" Mrs. Diederik put her hands on her daughter's shoulders. "I'm so sorry."

"No, it's all good." Ahri smiled at Lessa. "Kayn and I are only part Korean. He looks it more than I do. Someday you'll learn about how genes work, and it'll make more sense. Green eyes aren't very common among our mother's people, but her grandfather was from Australia and had light eyes." Ahri didn't like to talk about him. He'd just been another man who'd acted like he loved a Korean woman and then left her. Maybe that was a curse on the women of her family. The men never stayed.

"That's Nikolas over there playing with Ezreal," Francie said.

"You have beautiful children, Mrs. Diederik."

"Oh, heavens, call me Francie." She glanced around the room. "Supper's ready."

Once again, Ahri held back as the others went into the large dining room. She glanced around the place, impressed by the attention to detail on the stained beams. The subtle yet bright colors on the walls lit up what could have been a dark room.

The only empty chair at the table was between Kayn and Rafe. When she reached for it, Rafe jumped up and pulled it out for her. Kayn shot him a quizzical look— because why would a brother ever get a chair for his sister? Ahri had to bite back a smile.

She didn't take part in the various conversations but simply enjoyed the comfortable banter. Darius was asking Alex his opinion about some of their weapons designs, while Francie and Kayn talked about the garden.

Rafe and Ezreal were going on about the music. When the musician realized she was watching them, his face colored, and he stumbled over his words in a stutter. He snapped his mouth shut and his food seemed to steal his attention.

Kayn had mentioned that Ezreal had stuttered as a child and was self-conscious about it. She'd asked her brother how the man led a team of musicians, including women. Evidently, once he knew he was safe around someone, he did just fine. Poor man. Somehow, Ahri had to help him see her as safe.

She made sure not to look his way again, not wanting to make him uncomfortable. The children were now laughing at something their father had said. The people in the room—except for her—had a sense of connection. It was a sweet feeling to be around them. That was the only word she could think of for it—a sense of *family*. No wonder Kayn was so happy here. On the ride over, he'd raved about what a great place it was.

She glanced around the room again. It was so much more than simply a house. Growing up, a house had been all her mother had been able to provide, too consumed with the grief of being abandoned. She'd gone to work every morning only because Ahri had made her get up and be the adult. By the time Ahri had married, she'd been confident that her mother could at least take care of herself physically. How to help her find happiness alone had been a different thing altogether.

Ahri shifted away from such a negative thought. It wasn't like she'd done any better in choosing a husband.

After dinner and the cleanup, they played a few games that the children could take part in. Even Ezreal participated, though Ahri sensed that he glanced at her a lot. She was careful to keep her eyes on others in the room, letting her peripheral vision follow him. Did he know that he actually brought more attention to himself when he did that?

More than once, she caught Rafe watching Ez and shaking his head at him. Ahri's gaze met Rafe's, and she had to cover her mouth to keep from laughing. She determined then to make Ezreal as comfortable around her as he was with Francie.

When everyone was ready to leave for the evening, Ahri held back. Her brother glanced at her.

"You sure you're okay with this?" he asked.

"Oh, yes." She glanced around the room and sighed. "This is perfect for me. You don't have to worry."

"Give me a shout if you need anything." He gave her a quick hug and bounded down the steps to his car. Darius went right behind him, waving as he left. Ezreal had to extricate himself from the children before he could follow.

"If you find there's anything you left at the complex," Rafe said, stepping next to her, "let me know.

Ma reminded me that I need to take more time for myself. I'll try to swing by a couple of times a week to get away from the office."

"She told you that, and you *listened?*" Ahri couldn't help teasing him. In some ways, his obsession with work reminded her too much of her brother. She'd have to ask Francie about it and see if it was possible to convince Kayn to do the same thing. Ahri understood that they had a deadline to meet, so she'd be patient until then.

"Sometimes I do, especially when she's right." He put his hands in his pockets and skipped down the steps to his car.

Ahri thought the visit had invigorated him. In fact, thinking back, she decided all the guys had left lighter of step than when they'd arrived.

"I'll take your luggage upstairs for you." Alex picked up her bags and headed up the stairs.

"I hope you like your room," Francie said. "It's the only one in the gable and has a lovely view."

"Thank you for letting me stay here."

"Thank me tomorrow after we've worked in the garden for a few hours." Francie indicated they should go up the stairs.

"You have a beautiful home." Ahri glanced around, wondering what it'd looked like when they'd been poor. "I love your taste in decorating."

"Some of that comes from Alex," Francie said. "He's the historian. We found some old photos in the attic from when my great grandparents lived here. A lot of our ideas came from those. It's too bad I wasn't able to keep their wonderful antiques."

"You had to sell them?"

"Yes. I suppose Rafe already told you. He doesn't mind people knowing he hasn't always been rich." She pointed to a photo on the wall. "This was from high school when he thought he wanted to swim competitively."

"Wanted to?" Ahri stepped closer. She'd know those brown eyes anywhere. His younger self looked up at the camera from the pool, his hair messed and dripping. "Didn't he stay with it?"

"No. The coach told him he had the enthusiasm and dedication but lacked one thing." His mother's eyes twinkled, evidently waiting for Ahri to guess. She shrugged, and Francie said, "Speed. He'd work so hard, but everyone was faster than him in the water."

"That's too bad." Ahri understood that frustration. "I always wanted to play basketball in high school. I was good at it but I lacked one thing." She shot Francie a sidelong glance.

"Height?" Rafe's mother said with a chuckle.

"Exactly."

"You're taller than I am."

"Not by much. Kayn got our father's height, but I inherited our mother's. I was so happy when I discovered the Petite section at the thrift store."

When Ahri had gone up a few more steps, she noticed a painting of the house. She glanced back at Francie, her brows raised.

"That's one I couldn't bring myself to sell." Francie ran a loving hand down the frame. "We're slowly replacing pictures. Alex is quite the sleuth. It takes time because we're not rich, but I think that makes it more fun." Her expression clouded. "My two youngest children are experiencing a much different childhood from the one Rafe had."

It didn't sound like that was a bad thing.

"Well, here's your room."

Ahri followed her hostess inside. The decor was very different from some of the colorful rooms downstairs. It was less fashionable and had a log cabin feel to it. The wood beams on the ceiling had a lighter stain, and the walls were cream-colored. That let the colorful patchwork quilt on the bed take center focus.

"This is beautiful." Ahri touched the fabric, noting the individual hand stitches.

"It was a wedding gift from my Granny Gladys, the only present we received from anyone in my family." Francie ran her hand over it.

The only wedding present Francie had received? The sadness in her hostess's eyes kept Ahri from asking about it. At least Zed's family had come to the wedding, though it'd been obvious they'd only done it for show. Francie must only be in her early forties and been right out of high school when she'd married Rafe's father.

"Granny left me this place. She's the one who'd wanted to make it into a bed-and-breakfast." Francie gave a soft sigh. "It's been fun to bring her dream to life."

"It's a beautiful room."

"Thank you. Now, about tomorrow." Francie crossed her arms. "I usually like to get as much done as possible in the morning when Alex and the children are in school."

"I warn you I've not had much experience with gardening, but I'm a quick study. It'll be nice to have something productive to do." Ahri rubbed her temples. "I've had too much free time the last few days."

"Free time to think about things you're not ready to."

"Yes." Ahri couldn't keep the sadness from her voice.

"I'll keep you busy then." Francie gave her a one-armed hug. "Make yourself at home here. Let me know if you're missing anything. Our guests frequently forget important things like toothpaste, so we keep a supply on hand. Good night."

Ahri put the glass case with her mother's Korean doll in the center of the dresser. Having that in place already made her feel like she was home.

She took her time unpacking. Funny that she'd just done it a few days ago at Kayn's place. Why had that seemed more like staying in a hotel than this did? She tried the bed and found it a comfortable fit for her back.

Yes. Now, if she could stop worrying that she'd still heard nothing from or about Zed, she thought she should enjoy it here.

Chapter 7

A hri stretched in the comfortable bed, testing her hamstrings. After three days of gardening, the worst of the over-used muscle aches had decreased. She'd always exercised back home but must not have used the same muscles. When she'd tried to get out of bed the second day, she'd hardly been able to move. Gardening, it seemed, was a great form of exercise.

She hadn't understood how much work helping with the garden would be, things like hauling wheelbarrows full of compost, pushing a Rototiller, hoeing the rows, setting up drip lines. She'd even gotten a little sunburned because she hadn't been careful the first day. The size of the garden had intimidated her, but she found she enjoyed the hard work. When she finally had her own place again, she thought she'd like a garden, though much smaller than Francie's.

The sound of the children rising drifted up to her room, with Nik squealing about something Lessa had done. The Diederiks were laid back as parents. Did that come because they were older? Francie had mastered a stern look that brought her children into line, while Alex had a way of teasing his children out of their temper tantrums.

For a second Ahri wondered what kind of parents she and Zed would have been. She pushed the thought aside. It didn't matter. Now that she'd seen this style of parenting, she knew this was what she wanted to be like. If she ever had a family of her own. Hopefully she wouldn't end up like her mother, unable to let go and move on.

At dinner, Alex talked about the history classes he taught at the college. This weekend he was hosting an end-of-term guillotine party for his Revolution in History class. Ahri wished she'd had fun teachers like him when she'd been in college. She might have stuck with her general studies and then finally chosen a major.

She went to the gable window that overlooked the property and surveyed the grounds, as she did every morning. The weather here was definitely muggier than she'd been used to in Arizona. Summer might be a bit much, but the B&B had air conditioning for hot days, so it shouldn't be too bad. She paused at the thought. Would she be there for the summer? Maybe.

Showered, her hair in a ponytail, and dressed for work in jeans and a T-shirt, Ahri skipped down the stairs. She picked up Nik, hugged him, and then chewed on his belly, making him squeal. His sister scurried over, her arms outstretched for her morning hug.

Zed hadn't grown up in a demonstrative family, and he hadn't liked much touching outside of the bedroom. Ahri's parents had been better about it, mostly her mother. It'd probably been the one parenting thing she'd been really good at. Until Ahri had experienced the Diederik family, she hadn't realized how starved for touch she'd been.

"What can I do to help this morning?" she asked, entering the kitchen.

"If you would be a dear and get the oatmeal going for those two, I'd appreciate it." Francie gave her the usual one-armed hug before going back to packing a sack lunch for her husband. She did that for him every day.

"Have you gotten the results for your online test?" Ahri asked as she took down a pot from a hook on the wall.

"I got an A." Francie's cheeks flushed, and she looked proud.

"When do you graduate?"

"At this rate I might be eighty when I finally walk."

Ahri considered that as she waited for the water to boil. She knew that Francie had cut back from a full schedule because of the children.

"Do you resent only being able to take one class a semester?"

"Oh, heavens no." Francie closed the lid on the lunch box. "I have the best of both worlds now. I've always wanted to graduate from college, so I signed up once Rafe went to Harvard. The local college accepted me for an employment program for women returning to the school. I was assigned to the history department."

"History?" Ahri grinned. "So Alex was one of the professors in your department."

"He was *my* professor. I worked for him." Francie colored again. "Once we started dating, I went to work for one of the other professors in the department. The first time Alex came to the house, I was so surprised I fell off the roof."

Ahri blinked, thinking of the pitch of the B&B's roof. She couldn't imagine climbing on it, much less falling from it. "Were you hurt very badly?"

"I only sprained my ankle because Alex broke my fall with his chest." She burst out laughing. "He must have had the *worst* bruise from my boot, but he'd never admit it to me."

"*Guys,*" Ahri said, stirring the now-bubbling oatmeal. "All their macho gets in the way of showing a flaw." She wondered if that'd been part of the reason Zed had never confided in her about what he was up to.

104

"What about macho men?" Alex pulled Francie into his arms and kissed her.

She shot Ahri a quick glance, and both women laughed.

He turned to face Ahri, one arm still around his wife's shoulders. "Why do I have the feeling that you two were talking about *me*?"

"We were." Francie handed him his lunch. "About your first visit here."

"When she screamed and came sliding off the roof. . ." He kissed her temple. "I thought I'd killed her."

"You saved me." Francie gave her husband such a look of love that Ahri had to glance away, her eyes prickling.

She focused her attention on the food. Had she ever looked at Zed like that? He'd certainly never looked at her that way. Her heart ached a little. What had she and Zed had then, besides attraction? Looking back on it now, she wondered what they could have been thinking to get married.

Some of the cryptic remarks about Francie's first husband came to mind and the horrible home life he'd created. The man couldn't have been anything like Alex. Poor, tenderhearted Francie to have been tied to such an unkind man. Why had she stayed with him?

Ahri paused, a little surprised at how far her view on the subject had changed. Her father's desertion had left her little-girl mind with a rigid belief that couples should always stay together to work out their problems. She'd amended that to exclude physical abuse. When she'd first considered leaving Zed, guilt had eaten at her. She'd thought she must be no better than her father if she were willing to destroy her family. How wrong she'd been.

After she turned off the burner and moved the pot to the back of the stove, she went into the living room where the children were playing with their toys in the corner.

"Your breakfast is almost done. Do you have everything ready for school, Lessa?"

The girl jumped up and ran to grab her little backpack. She thrust it at Ahri before returning to the toys on the floor. She enjoyed the two little ones and their precocious personalities, but they did test her patience sometimes. Ahri hadn't had a lot of experience with children in recent years. She'd stopped babysitting when she'd turned sixteen and could get a better-paying job. They'd needed the extra money to pay the bills.

Alex strode into the room carrying his briefcase. He set it down and swung both of his children. They squealed at his kisses.

If they'd had any children, Ahri couldn't imagine Zed behaving like this. This was what she wanted in her future, a man who wasn't afraid to touch and tease, to show his love and regard.

"Thank you so much for the help you've been this week," Alex said.

Ahri pulled herself from her thoughts to find he'd set down the children and picked up his briefcase again.

"It's been fun." Cathartic, though she didn't say it aloud.

"Well, it's helped Francie a lot and taken a load off my mind. She keeps insisting on enlarging the garden." He sent a fond glance toward the kitchen before saying to his children, "You two clean this up and then eat your breakfast."

"Bye, daddy."

Under his watchful eye, they started picking up the toys. He winked at Ahri and strode out to his car.

Ahri evaluated what she'd need for the drip system on the section she'd prepped. She wiped the sweat from her brow. Her appetite had been good with all the work she'd been doing. Her stomach growled. She was already looking forward to dinner. It would be at least another hour before Francie got back from taking Lessa to her piano lesson, and Ahri would need to clean up so she could help prepare for dinner.

The sound of tires on the gravel driveway drifted to the back of the house. The mail had already been delivered, and Francie's guests had mentioned being gone until early evening. Who could it be?

"Hey, Ma," Rafe's familiar voice yelled.

"She's not here," Ahri called, heading toward the house, surprised and pleased that he'd come in the middle of a workday.

Rafe came around the corner, dressed casually in jeans and a T-shirt rather than the business attire she'd have expected for this time of day. She wondered what he was there for.

"Well, dang. I'm sorry I missed her." Rafe came to stand by Ahri and glanced around. There ought to be a law against handsome men who smelled that good. He said, "I came to help with the garden."

"I won't complain." Ahri turned back to her row, biting back a grin.

"What have you got going there?" He followed her and scanned her work. "Nice job. You know, I think Ma must have doubled the size of this thing since I was in high school. Is she reckoning to sell at the farmer's market?"

"No. She said she's planning to expand the catering part of her business." Ahri fumbled with one of the connections for her line. "She said anything she doesn't use will go to the local food pantry."

"That sounds like my mother. Let me show you something." Rafe took the two pieces and brought them together. "If you pinch it like this, it'll slide right in." He handed it back to her.

Ahri made a disgusted sound. "I wish you'd been here earlier this week. I've been struggling for days."

"Didn't Ma tell you?"

She thought back. "I don't think she's been out here with me since I started this part."

"Where do you want me to work?" he asked.

"That section over there needs compost before we can till it in."

"All right."

Ahri watched while he went to the full wheelbarrow and dumped it before heading back to the pile of compost near the driveway for more. Since he'd spent years helping with the garden, she'd have expected him to want to start bossing her around. That was unexpected, a CEO who didn't have to always be in charge.

She tried not to look at him while he worked, but she found herself glancing his way often. Rafe seemed to know what he needed to do and went right at it. From the way his back and arm muscles pressed against his T-shirt as he shoveled the compost, he must work out. Kayn had mentioned the complex having an employee gym. She didn't know if the CEO would use it with everyone else. Maybe he had his own equipment in his apartment there. No one could look *that* good naturally. For a man who spent so much time in his office, he was in really good shape.

Ahri frowned. She shouldn't be admiring the way he looked.

"What do you like to do when you're not working?" she asked to get her mind on something else. "I mean, besides helping your mother with her garden."

"I game, of course."

"Don't we all?" Not that she'd played since coming to Francie's.

"I read." He glanced into the distance. "I write."

Since she'd been looking at him again, she saw his neck darken, like he was embarrassed.

"You mean besides the champion lore?"

Rafe shifted his feet. He did write more than stuff for the game. How cool was that?

"What are you writing?" she asked.

"Nothing much. Just a story I've been messing around with."

"Will you tell me more?" she asked.

"It's a political thriller." He didn't look at her. "I wanted to try something different from the game fantasy. I don't have much time to work on it. I don't think I've opened the file in months."

"How fun. Not the part where you haven't looked at it lately." Ahri sensed he didn't want to say more, so she went back for additional supplies. A political thriller. That was so different from the fantasy lore that he'd been writing. She wondered what kind of research he'd have to do for something like that.

"What kind of music are you into?" she asked when he came back with another load of compost.

"Why do you ask?" Rafe watched her, his head tilted to the side.

"Just making conversation."

"All right. I like all kinds now. I grew up with country but you can imagine how well that was received at Harvard. I broadened my tastes out of self-defense."

Seeing this side of Rafe Davis was turning the image Ahri'd had of him upside down. The polished, almost suave, front man for REKD Gaming was very different from this version who was shoveling compost for his mother's garden. She found him intriguing. Which was he, the country boy or the sophisticated businessman?

"What about you?" He wiped at his brow, now glistening with perspiration.

"Oh, me?" She fumbled with the parts in her hands, not realizing she'd stopped working. "I like a lot of different kinds too, but especially ones with girl soloists."

"Girl power music?" he asked, a glint of humor in his expression.

"I guess, though I hadn't really thought about it that way."

"Are you a cat person or a dog person?"

She grinned. "I'm allergic to cats, so by default I'm a dog person. I think, anyway. We weren't able to have pets when I was growing up. We always lived in apartments and couldn't afford to pay the pet deposit. I used to beg my mother for a puppy when I was little."

"I never had a dog either. My father was sensitive to loud noises. Barking dogs upset him too much. I can't tell you how many times he called the police about our neighbor's dog."

So he hadn't been allowed a dog either. Ahri hadn't expected to have so much in common with this man. She wondered if they also had name issues.

"Is Rafe your name or a nickname?" she asked.

"Nickname. My name's Raphael."

"Like the painter?"

"I got teased because of the mutant turtle," Rafe said, making a face.

She burst out laughing. "Children can be so mean about names."

"It's not just kids." Rafe shook his head. "There was a guy in our dorm who thought he was so clever and kept asking where Kayn's brother was."

Ahri shrugged, not getting the joke.

"The guy would then ask where Abel was."

"Oh." She gave a snort of disgust. "That's lame. Kayn never mentioned that."

"I'm sure he didn't. I finally started riding the guy for his lack of creativity and told him his joke was as old as the hills and twice as dusty."

"And he stopped?"

"When everyone on our floor started calling him Dusty, yeah."

"That's awesome," she said, chuckling. "I could never get anybody to spell mine right. The one thing our father did was let our mother name us, and she wanted our names to be unique. I had a second-hand bike and dearly wanted one of those toy license plates with my name on it. Even now, you'll never see my spelling on any of the display cases."

"It's pretty," Rafe said.

Ahri's face warmed with pleasure. His open admiration unsettled her, and she had to focus on her hands again.

"What kinds of things do you have on your bucket list?" he asked.

Ahri stared off at the trees in the distance. "I'm not sure I have one right now. I just want to get through the next few weeks."

Rafe was about to ask Ahri what those plans were, when her phone rang. There were only a handful of people who knew the number to the special phone Bill had given her.

She frowned at the screen, her face going pale, and she seemed hesitant to accept the call.

"Something wrong?" Rafe stepped closer.

"It says it's from the Phoenix police."

In spite of the sun's heat, a chill of worry ran down Rafe's back. His protective instincts triggered, and he moved beside her.

She shot him a worried glance and accepted the call.

"Hello?" she asked, her voice hesitant, wary. "Yes, this is Ahri Meisner."

Rafe wished he could hear what the other person was saying.

"Yes, I have someone with me."

The memory of the other time he'd heard that same question asked of his mother set all his mental alarms off. Had Zed *died*?

Rafe put a bracing arm around Ahri's shoulders just in time. She jerked and her knees gave out. He eased her to the ground, and she buried her face in her raised knees. Dropping beside her, he picked up the phone and made sure the call hadn't been disconnected. He put it on speaker.

"My name's Rafe Davis. I'm a family friend."

"This is Officer Warwick of the Phoenix Police Department. I'm afraid I have bad news. Mr. Meisner's body was found yesterday."

Just what he'd been afraid of. "Do you think it was foul play?" Rafe asked.

"It appears likely."

Beside him, Ahri stirred.

"Is Mrs. Meisner in any danger?" Rafe asked, and she straightened.

"Possibly," the officer said. "It'd be wise to assume she is, as a precaution."

"*I'm* in danger?" she asked, her voice soft.

"He said it's just a precaution." Rafe didn't want to treat her like a child, but he didn't want to overwhelm her either.

"Yes, just a precaution," Officer Warwick agreed. "You're aware she left the state to stay with her brother after the break-in."

"Yes, she informed us."

"I'll have my head of security get in touch with you."
Rafe waited for the inevitable question.

"Your head of security?"

"I own a business in the state where she's staying."
Rafe didn't know why his gut told him to play it close
about Ahri's whereabouts. Maybe he'd seen too many
movies where the local police had a leak. Regardless, he
didn't think it necessary to offer information that might
put her in danger. "Here's my number. My guy's name is
Bill Ryze, and you'll be hearing from him."

"I'll look forward to his call." Warwick disconnected
the call.

Rafe put down the phone, not sure what to say. He
forced his shoulder muscles to relax because they'd
started to cramp. He wanted to offer her comfort,
support. *Something.* And Kayn needed to know.

Before Rafe could reach for his phone, Ahri leaned
her head against his shoulder. He put his arms around
her again, and she turned into his chest, crying at last. He
held her, feeling helpless. Weren't there some magical
words out there that would help ease her pain? He
remembered all the platitudes people had said to him
and his mother after his father's death.

Ahri's husband had been *murdered.* Had whoever'd
done that gotten what they needed from the apartment,
or had the neighbor interrupted the search before they
found it? Could she really be in danger now?

"Please tell me this is a nightmare." She
straightened, wiping her eyes.

115

"I wish I could." Rafe brushed aside a strand of hair from her cheek.

"I just don't understand. Why would anyone kill a lowly CPA?" Ahri looked up into the sky like she was seeking help from the heavens. "He kept *books*, for heaven's sake."

"I know. If he had a gambling debt—you *did* say you were worried about that, didn't you?" When she nodded, he said, "It wouldn't make sense to kill him," he said.

Ahri nodded and rubbed her temples, a crease between her brows.

"We need to let Kayn and Bill know about this." Rafe dialed the number, the phone still on speaker.

"I was about to call you," Ryze said without a greeting.

"I'm at my mother's with Ahri." Rafe explained about the call from the police.

Bill swore softly. "That makes my news even worse."

"What?" Rafe and Ahri said at the same time.

"The truck with her things has disappeared."

She went even paler, her mouth forming a small *o*.

"Like *stolen*?" Rafe asked.

"Apparently. They notified Kayn since he's the one who contracted with them," Bill said. "Did they say how long Meisner's been dead?"

"I didn't think to ask," Rafe said, irritated with himself.

"That man who was watching the packers," Ahri said suddenly.

"Right. Bill, I need you to contact the Phoenix police about this." Rafe gave him the officer's information. "Where's Kayn now?"

"Just went into a brainstorming meeting."

Rafe met Ahri's gaze and could tell she was going to say not to bother her brother. "He'll want to be told now, so he can be here with you."

She heaved out a breath. "All right."

"Do you need anything else from me, Bill?" Rafe asked.

"No. I'll get right on it." Bill paused. "I'm sorry about your husband, Mrs. Meisner."

"Should we have her use a different last name?" Rafe asked.

"Not a bad idea. Rafe, you'll need to explain to your folks about what's going on," Bill said.

"Ahri, had you considered going back to your maiden name or did you reckon to keep his?" Rafe asked.

"I hadn't thought that far ahead." She leaned her head against his shoulder again.

Her touch made Rafe hyperaware of the contact. He ached to do something more for her.

"Since we don't know what kind of people your husband was involved with," Bill said, "it might be best to put some distance between your names. Does your husband have any family in Arizona?"

"Yes, but they were awful to me because of me being part Korean," she said with a sniff. "I haven't seen any of them in a couple of years."

"This may seem a little premature," Bill said, his voice kind, "but you need to think about funeral arrangements. I should state right now that I'm opposed to you attending."

"Not go to his funeral?" Ahri's voice had gone quiet. "He was my husband."

"Your estranged husband, yes," Bill said.

Rafe's first thought had been that it was her husband's fault for having gotten himself into this and he'd managed to drag her into it too. But he had to accept that even though the marriage would have ended anyway, her feelings about her late husband weren't black and white.

"I agree with Bill," Rafe said, gently. "It's not like Zed died in a car crash."

"I *know* he was mur—dered." She choked on the word. "How can I not go?"

"To keep you safe." Rafe's heart ached for her, and he wrapped an arm around her again.

"But, why? I don't *know* anything."

"They might not realize that. I think Rafe's right," Bill said. "For your own safety, you need to stay in North Carolina, out of sight. I'll get to work." He ended the call.

"Do you want to tell Kayn?" Rafe asked, leaving the *Or should I?* implied.

"You, please."

Rafe's stomach was in a knot. He wanted to hit something. They'd brought Ahri here to *protect* her, but there was no way to protect her from the pain of her husband being murdered. He would need to talk to Bill about increasing the security at the B&B.

Chapter 8

"Wow, that was even harder than I expected," Kayn said, still kneeling by Ahri's chair after they'd hung up from the phone call to their mother. "I'm glad you didn't tell her *how* he died."

When Ahri's eyes welled with tears again, he pulled her into another embrace. She was so glad he'd been there with her. What would she have done if she'd still been alone in Arizona when she'd received the news?

At least telling her mother hadn't been as traumatic as talking to Zed's sister had been. The police had already informed them, and the family was making plans for the funeral. Not surprisingly, she'd made it clear Ahri need not attend. Even expecting that response, it still hurt.

"I still think you should come back to my suite," Kayn said when she stopped crying.

"I need to have people around. It's better for me here." As long as Francie was agreeable, Ahri meant to stay there, at least until she knew what she was going to do next—and as long as her presence posed no danger to the Diederiks.

At the sound of cars pulling up outside, Kayn rose. Francie had suggested the guys be invited for dinner. Ahri's hostess was understanding and intuitive, maybe because she'd also lost a husband. She must have realized that Ahri would have retreated if left to her own devices.

"They're here," he said. "You sure you're up to this meeting after the meal?"

Ahri nodded and pulled more tissues from the box by her bed. "I have to be."

Kayn held out a hand. She took it, and he pulled her to her feet. He slid her arm through his, and they went down the stairs together.

Ahri sat quietly at the dinner table, grateful everyone kept up a lively discussion, all about work. Their passion for what they did made a good distraction. She thought back on the emotional call to her mother and heaved a sigh.

"How are you holding up?" Rafe whispered.

"I wish I could go to sleep for a month, so this would all be over." She moved the mostly uneaten food around her plate. "My mother's emotionally fragile, and it was hard to tell her he was gone. She liked Zed a lot."

Rafe's mother reached over and gave Ahri's hand a squeeze. Francie *would* understand.

"Well," Darius said, rising and picking up his plate, "another fantastic meal, Mrs. D. I believe Ez and I will take the little ones out back while you have your meeting with Bill." He grinned at Nik. "I brought some finger paints, Ace."

"Yes!" The young boy threw both arms in the air.

"I brought a recorder," Ezreal's voice was soft as he looked at Lessa, "in case you want me to teach you how to play it too, since you're learning to read music now." It was the most Ahri had heard him say at one time.

"We'll look forward to the Chess Pie after," Darius said. "Bring your plate with you Nik."

Lessa picked up hers and hurried after the artist. Ez shot Ahri a sympathetic glance before he followed the others. Had the shy man actually looked at her on purpose? The rest of the adults quickly cleaned up the meal and went into the living room where Rafe had set up his laptop.

"Don't feel obligated to include us," Alex said, his arm around Francie's shoulders. "We don't want to intrude."

"If I'm going to stay here, you'll need to know what's going on. You already feel like family." Ahri rubbed her cold hands together. "I appreciate your support."

"Are you ready?" Rafe asked.

She nodded.

"Is everyone here that you want to be part of this, Ahri?" Bill asked as soon as his face appeared on the screen.

"Yes," she said. "Is there no way to keep me safe if I go to the funeral?"

"Why should you bother to go after they said you weren't welcome?" Kayn asked, his face tight.

"Because it would prove to them that I *did* love him."

"You're still trying to prove yourself to them?" Kayn's tone was incredulous. He'd never liked Zed and had done a poor job of hiding it. While her mother had been charmed by him, her brother hadn't forgiven him for not standing up to his family's poor treatment of Ahri.

"I'd like to honor what we had in the beginning."

"I completely understand," Francie said with a meaningful glance at Rafe, who was frowning.

"But if there's any chance you could be in danger, you shouldn't go," Kayn said.

"What if there's another way?" Francie asked in her quiet voice.

"What do you have in mind, Mrs. Diederik?" Bill asked.

"Well, what if it only *looks* like she's there?"

"What?" Kayn asked. "How?"

"Wait." Rafe raised a hand. "I think I know where my mother's going with this. What if we hire an actress to pretend to be Ahri? Bill could put together a team to film the funeral and keep an eye out on who attends. That way she could still watch it without being there." He glanced at Ahri. "Didn't you say they haven't seen you in a couple of years?"

She nodded, the idea intriguing.

"Your stand-in could wear a black veil," Alex suggested.

"Isn't that kind of old school?" Kayn asked.

"Women sometimes still wear veils," Francie said, "especially to honor a husband."

"I like the idea, but I won't put the actress in danger instead of me." Ahri put as much force in her voice as she could.

"Bill would arrange security," Rafe said. "I've had to do this before, for myself. It was right after we sold the first game and were all over the news. Being the CEO, I was the front man."

"He ended up with a stalker," Bill added.

"Oh, yeah." Kayn nodded. "I'd almost forgotten about that."

"Lucky you," Rafe said, his tone flat.

"You never told me that." Francie sent her son a disapproving look.

"That's because he had me to take care of it." Bill shifted his gaze to Ahri. "We'll make sure the actress is safe. But, I have another suggestion that would go along with the funeral ruse."

The others who'd started talking, quieted.

DONNA K. WEAVER

"I'd like to set up a decoy in a luxury apartment in New York where Kayn owns property," Bill said

"My condo?" her brother asked.

"You mean your penthouse," Rafe said.

"You bought a penthouse?" Ahri asked, shocked. Maybe because she'd never accepted financial help from him, the magnitude of his wealth hadn't sunk in.

"Hey, it's an investment." Kayn shrugged. "The REKD North American finals are held at Madison Square Garden."

"The four of us stayed there last year," Rafe added, "and hosted a party with Esports bigwigs who could rub shoulders with city officials and our sponsors. It's not being used this time of year."

"Wouldn't this decoy woman be in danger?" Ahri asked.

"I don't think they want to hurt you so much as search your possessions," Bill said." I know of a young woman who's a criminology student in Maryland. She's been working part-time in a private investigator's office, so she has some practical experience. I've spoken with her, and she'd be happy to do this as a paid internship. Now, do bear in mind that this might all be for nothing. Whoever stole the truck might have found what they were looking for.

"She'll travel to the funeral under your name—your maiden name. The apartment's already in your brother's name. Anyone who might be following her after the funeral will find her at the apartment. She wouldn't go

126

out much, but when she did, she'd have a bodyguard. My goal is to keep their attention focused on that penthouse and away from Boone." Bill glanced at Kayn. "I assume you're not worried about expenses."

"No. I've got this. I like the idea," her brother said.

"What do you think?' Francie asked Ahri.

"I know you're worried for me," she said to Kayn, and he gave her one of his *duh* looks. Remembering her sister-in-law's chilling tone, she said to Bill, "You'll have to warn your decoy that she won't have a good reception from his family at the funeral."

"I guess that means you're okay with this?" Rafe asked.

"I can live with it," Ahri said.

"All right. I'll set it up. Did they tell you when it is?" Bill asked.

"No, but I found the notice online," Ahri said. "I'll send you a link."

She was rubbing her hands again. Rafe took one and held it between his. His skin warmed more than her hands, sending an unexpected pulse through her. It made her feel alive again, in a way she hadn't in years.

"Ahri, are you listening?" Kayn asked, pulling her back.

"I'm sorry," she said, still a little distracted. "What were you saying?" Rafe had released the one hand but took the other, seemingly unconcerned at the way her brother was watching him. She pulled back her hand.

"Bill was asking if you've decided on a new last name," her brother said.

"He didn't like me going back to my maiden name because of the connection to you. Since most Whites can't tell Asians apart, I'll be Ahri Shen." She glanced at Kayn, waiting for his reaction.

"*Chinese?*" He spewed the word out like it tasted bad.

"Don't be racist." Ahri rolled her eyes. "My best friend in second grade's last name was Shen."

"Good reasoning," Bill said. "What do you plan in the short term?"

"What *can* I do? It's not like I have ID for a new identity." Ahri couldn't keep the bitterness from her voice. She hated feeling helpless, having to rely on the charity of others, as kind as they might be about it.

"We'll get this figured out soon," Kayn assured her, seeming to understand her feelings.

"*How* soon?" Ahri couldn't stop the flow of words. "I'm in limbo here, you know. I can't go anywhere. I can't even get a *job*." She shot a quick look at Francie. "I'm grateful for the way you've opened your home to me. I love being here and helping you with your garden in exchange for my room and board, so I mean no offense."

"None taken." Francie nodded in understanding. "You're preaching to the choir, honey. I understand the need to work and be productive, to be in control of your life. I'm sure we'll figure something out."

Rafe was watching her, his eyes narrowed like he was thinking about something.

"What?" Ahri asked.

"What was your job before?"

"I was an executive assistant. Why?"

"Olaf's gone to law school, and we haven't found a replacement yet." Rafe shifted his gaze to Kayn. "My other assistant is going on maternity leave soon."

"Great idea. My sister's the queen of organization." Her brother grinned. "I'll bet she'd give even Olaf a run for his money."

"What do you think?" Rafe asked Ahri.

"What about your HR people? They're going to want my birth certificate and stuff to prove I can legally work in the US."

"Bill, do you think we can trust Orianna with it?"

"Yes. She wouldn't be in her position if she didn't have great discretion."

"All right then." Rafe looked back at Ahri. "You can start when you're ready. It's just a temp job, if you want it."

"*Yes.*" She had to force herself not to throw her arms around his neck.

"Yo, Rafe, wait up." Kayn jogged up to him outside of the complex entrance.

Rafe stopped, his hands in his pockets, and waited for the inevitable. He'd expected some kind of response after the way Kayn had been staring at him. The simple act of warming Ahri's hands had been in response to the way she'd kept rubbing them together. It'd been obvious to him that she'd needed physical contact at the moment, and her brother hadn't been providing it.

It'd have been presumptuous to lecture Kayn about it, not knowing what kind of home they'd been raised in. Having grown up with a cold father but a loving, demonstrative mother, Rafe knew how to recognize a need for touch when he saw it.

While he hadn't expected the physical jolt it'd given him, it hadn't surprised him either. He'd been attracted to Ahri since the first time he'd met her just before she'd gotten engaged to Zed.

Rafe hadn't really thought about what he'd meant by warming her hands. He knew it was a tough time for her. He had no intention of taking advantage of her vulnerability, but he'd been thinking about her a lot. Three years ago he hadn't been ready, but his mother was right. It was time to move on from that disaster with Tess. When Ahri was in a good place again, he wasn't going to hold back this time.

"What's up?" Rafe asked.

"What was that you were pulling with my sister?" Kayn's tone had a joking quality to it, but it also had an edge.

"You mean offering her a job?" Rafe kept his face neutral.

"Don't play stupid with me." Kayn grasped his shoulder. "What's going on?"

"I was just warming her hands. Nothing's going on." Rafe paused before adding, " *Yet.*"

Kayn gave him a flat look.

"And nothing might happen, so don't worry. For right now, all I want is to be her friend."

"For right now. That's good since you're going to be her boss."

Rafe frowned, having forgotten that little problem. It'd been an issue for his mother and Alex too. He'd been one of the professors she'd worked for. At the college, they didn't allow supervisors to date anyone under them, and neither did REKD Gaming. It was good policy. Rafe couldn't take special privileges for himself just because he was the CEO, especially not for someone under his direct supervision.

For a second, he wished he hadn't offered her the position. But no. She needed time to heal anyway, and the temporary job would be perfect for that.

"Come *on,*" Kayn said, interrupting, "what's going through that brilliant brain of yours?"

"First of all, regarding your sister, it's premature. Her husband hasn't even been buried yet."

"She's been falling out of love with him for a couple of years. She only hung in there so long out of loyalty to the vows she made, not to the man." Kayn's expression had turned so earnest, that Rafe laughed.

"A minute ago you were challenging me for being interested in your sister and now you're telling me to go ahead?"

"Oh, shut up. It's timing and you know it. There couldn't be a better man for her than you."

"Timing. Yes, that's exactly what I was trying to tell you." Rafe held up his fingers as he spoke. "First, she has to bury her husband. Second, she needs time to recover from this. I have no intention of being a rebound. Third, there's the issue of me being her boss. It'll be good that we're friends first. Once Cass comes back from her maternity leave and this whole thing with Zed is resolved, Ahri can get another job. By then, she might be open to dating me. And if she's not, we'll still be friends. It wouldn't be the first time a woman didn't want me." Rafe pinched his lips closed. He hadn't meant to say anything about that.

"Why do you still let that bi—" Kayn bit back the word. "I know you were into Tess, but all of your friends—your real friends—saw what she was doing."

For two years, Rafe had refused to talk about her to any of them. He hadn't wanted to dredge up the pain. Thinking back to his mother's admonition, he realized that getting it in the open would be a step forward.

"And what was it you saw her doing with me?" he asked.

"Tess was never serious about you. I overheard her once at the campus bookstore just before she dumped you. She said she was 'slumming it' with you." Kayn shot him a sympathetic glance. "She played you and threw you to the curb like so much trash."

"Slumming it?" Rafe said, feeling a little numb. "She actually used those words?"

"Man, I'm sorry, but that's the truth."

Rafe rubbed the bridge of his nose. It hurt to hear it, but he wasn't surprised. A memory came back to him of the day the sale of their first game had hit the news, and they'd been labeled the Harvard Billionaire Boys.

"What are you grinning at?" Kayn asked.

"Did I ever tell you that Tess called and wanted to get back together?" Rafe gave a dark chuckle.

"Don't tell me it was after you got rich?"

"Yup." By then, he'd known what she was.

"I'd like to have been there when you had that little conversation," Kayn said a little too gleefully.

"Let's just say that the idea of getting back together with her stuck in my throat like a hair in a biscuit."

Kayn burst out laughing and clapped him on the back. "Good. As for you and my sister, I guess I'm okay with that. I wouldn't mind having you as my brother."

"You're jumping the gun." It was Rafe's turn to give a flat look. "We don't even know if Ahri will like me like that."

"All I saw was the look on her face when you were *warming her hand*, as you called it. I think when the time is right, there won't be any question about her wanting to date you. See ya." Grinning, Kayn jogged ahead.

Rafe watched him go, bemused. Maybe he was being an idiot to think of getting involved again. If his mother hadn't been pushing the issue, he might not have considered it. But there was also Ahri herself. He couldn't get her out of his thoughts. Once she'd moved to his mother's place, it'd been all he could do not to run out there every day to see how Ahri was, what her day had been like, to spend time with her. Rafe hadn't felt that way in a very long time, and he liked it. He tried to be pragmatic. They had time to see how things would play out.

Chapter 9

Two weeks later, Ahri arrived at the center to begin her training with Rafe's assistant, Cass. Kayn had fronted Ahri the money for a new wardrobe since the police had found the stolen truck burning in a field in Oklahoma. It and its contents had been a total loss.

That had led to another day spent crying. If she kept thinking that her precious things, the ones that could never be replaced, had been stolen by the same people who'd murdered her husband, she'd give herself an ulcer.

The time with Francie's family had helped. During the first days, they'd kept her distracted with their normalcy, and at night, Ahri had been able to grieve alone. Her tears had been for Zed's wasted life rather than the loss of their life together. She'd finally accepted that it had been dead for a long time.

When she saw Bill waiting at the main entrance, Ahri's stomach knotted. She doubted all new employees received an escort from the head of security. For such a nice man, he had a way of messing with her nervous system. Would he never have good news for her?

"Don't worry. It's not bad," he said with a chuckle as he extended his arm.

"Then you're not here to see me?" She shook his hand, the knot loosening a little.

"I am. I have some video I'd like you to look at."

"What of? That guy who was following me?" When he nodded, she said, "I'm here for training with Cass."

"I know. I sent her a message that you'll be late." He approached the central desk where a security guard watched him expectantly. "This is Ahri Shen. She'll be filling in for Cass while she's on maternity leave."

"Nice to meet you." The man handed her a guest badge. "HR will have your official tag when you attend your employee orientation meeting."

Ahri thought it was fortunate that Kayn hadn't introduced her around when she'd first arrived. Otherwise, showing up now with a different name and pretending *not* to be his sister would have been a problem.

Francie had taken Ahri shopping for work clothes and to a salon to learn to do her makeup differently.

Since she usually wore her long hair down, they'd opted to go for a sterner, pulled back look. It made her seem older. With heavier makeup and platform heels to make her taller, she wondered if her own mother would recognize her.

"This way," Bill said.

"This place is a labyrinth," she said once they reached the section designated as Security. "How often will I get lost?"

"Frequently, in the beginning, but you'll get used to it. Just ask anyone. They've all been through it." He said to the people working in cubicles, "This is the Ahri Shen that we've discussed." No one said anything, most merely giving her a nod in acknowledgement.

"They know about me?" she whispered.

"They have to. This way."

Inside of Bill's office, he indicated a chair and took his own. He turned one of his large monitors around so she could see the screen.

"These were from the night the moving truck was stolen." He clicked a button and the video started.

It looked like it'd been taken by an outside surveillance camera. The footage reminded Ahri of the kind on the news, dim and grainy. Recognizing the moving truck, she leaned closer. Three figures approached it, two keeping watch while one of them did something to the lock. She gave a little gasp at how quickly they got inside and had the truck started.

"I'm not too late." Rafe jogged into the office, a little breathless. "Kayn's in a meeting and asked me to come for him."

Ahri's heart gave a sharp little twist that made her wince. Her hand tingled at the memory of that incredibly intimate moment when Rafe had warmed her hands. She'd only seen him at Sunday dinners since, and he hadn't been particularly attentive. It was stupid that she was both glad—he *was* her boss now after all—and disappointed at the same time.

Rafe pulled up a chair besides hers. Ahri started to scoot away, but he put his hand over hers on the arm. "You're fine. What have we got here?" He dropped his hand and leaned forward.

"We're hoping Ahri can identify these men." Bill started the video again, and she shifted her attention back to the monitor. He must have put it on repeat because the short clip started again automatically. Neither man said anything as they scrutinized it.

"Can you play it slower?" she asked.

He touched something on his keyboard, and the images went into slow motion. She studied the man who'd played lookout. It seemed he must have known there could be a camera because he kept his face down, his head covered by a hoodie. At one point he turned his head sharply, perhaps at a sound, and exposed his face.

"Stop," she cried.

Bill had to move it back but then paused it at the right moment. Ahri felt queasy at the familiar face.

"That's *him*," she said, clenching the arms of her chair, "the guy who followed me. I don't recognize the other two."

Rafe gently covered her hand with his, and she relaxed her grip on the armrest. Once again, his touch calmed her.

"I'll let Officer Warwick know," Bill said.

"Do you think they found what they were looking for?" Rafe asked.

"Who knows?" Bill opened another screen. "I've got some more video from the funeral for you to view while you're here. Having several people filming it from different angles gave us a *lot* of footage to examine."

It had taken Ahri a week before she could watch the first video he'd sent over. She steeled herself to face it. Rafe laced his fingers over hers, and she let go of the chair, clinging to his hand instead, grateful for the support.

"You identified the family members and known friends or coworkers before," Bill said. "We've narrowed it down to these people."

Ahri watched closely, not recognizing any of them.

"They might be extended family that I never met," she said.

"Or business associates," Bill said.

"Of one kind or another," Rafe added, his voice soft.

Would the people who'd killed Zed have dared to come to his funeral? A shadow moved near a tree in the background. Ahri leaned in.

"What do you see?" Rafe asked, moving closer to the screen.

"Maybe nothing." She pointed to the tree line. "Is someone back there?"

Bill replayed it, slower this time. "Could be. One of my people marked it. Might just be a cemetery employee. I have my staff working to enhance it."

After the three of them had watched the videos enough times that Ahri's head hurt, Bill called an end.

"Did the decoy say if she thought she was being followed?" Rafe asked.

"Does she have a name?" Ahri asked. "Or are we always going to call her 'the decoy'?"

"Her name is Sona Rakan," Bill said. "To answer Rafe's question, she did spot someone following her. Since we had obvious security, no one made a move," Bill said. "On the trip back to New York, no one saw anyone who looked suspicious. I'll let you know if I have more," he said.

Ahri arched her back, only then aware that she was still holding Rafe's hand. She relaxed her fingers, and he did the same.

"It's not exactly the way you wanted to spend your first day at work," he said, standing. "Thanks for letting me be here."

"Thanks for being here." She resisted the pull to take his hand again and picked up her purse instead.

"I'm heading back to the office, so I can show you the way," Rafe said. "Keep me updated, Bill." He left the office, apparently expecting her to follow, so she did.

As Ahri and Rafe walked, she took in the familiar artwork on the hallway walls, all of REKD champions. The large pictures brought color and character to what would have been a long, sterile corridor. It finally opened on the left, exposing a large area full of work stations.

"This section has some of the engineers and production crews," Rafe said.

"It's really *open*." Ahri craned her neck, trying to figure out how many people were in what appeared to be a very congested area.

"That's the intent. This whole business is based on creativity. If someone has a question, it's easy to pop up and see if the people they need are at their stations. Others can chime in. It makes for some great synergy. The layout also fosters chance interactions that can lead to important discussions." Rafe grinned and continued down the hall. "It also cuts down on emails."

"Do you have a traditional office like Bill?"

"I do, but the guys and I also have stations like these." He shot her a sidelong glance. "Sometimes we need to be out in the thick of things too. Will that be a problem for you? When my mother came for a tour of the place, she said it'd drive her crazy."

"I'm used to working in a very traditional office." Ahri thought that her last job and this one must be on opposite ends of the spectrum. "I liked the quiet, so this will be an adjustment."

"It was for me too. I *am* my mother's son, after all."

And what a son he was. Ahri had been impressed with Rafe before, but as they continued, it surprised her how many people waved to him. He knew every one of them by name.

"How do you do it?" she asked softly.

"Do what? Learn to work in the chaos?"

"Know your employees so well. This is such a young company, and you've grown so fast. How can you keep track of everyone?"

"Don't tell anyone," he said conspiratorially, "but I have HR send me resumés and photos of all the new employees. I spend a little time each night going over files of the new people and refreshing my memory about others I don't interact with often. I can honestly say that I know everyone who works here."

"Wow. I'm . . ." Her words trailed off as she searched for the right word.

"Speechless?" He gave a dark chuckle. "My mother would say it's because I don't have a life."

"And you'd say this business *is* your life?" she asked softly.

He stopped and turned, those dark brown eyes piercing through her, like he could see into her mind.

"What?" she asked defensively, worried she'd offended him. "It's just what Kayn says when I tell him the same thing."

Rafe gave a soft grunt and strode toward another elevator.

"You aren't going to tell me?" Ahri hurried after him.

"I guess you can say all the Beta Boys have the same problem." He pushed the elevator button.

"The Beta Boys." She laughed, remembering the name of their original company.

"Now they call us the Billionaire Boys," Rafe said in a disgusted tone. "I liked the old name better."

The elevator opened to a very pregnant woman.

"Perfect timing." She stepped out. "Orianna has a list of applicants for you to review."

"Anyone look good?" He stepped into the elevator.

"A couple."

"I'll leave you in Cass's capable hands. See y'all later."

The door closed, and the woman turned to Ahri. "Welcome to REKD Gaming." She indicated a corridor to the right. "I'll give you a Cook's tour before we go back to our area. I'm Cass, by the way."

"Were your parents fans of that 1960s singer?" Ahri asked.

"I'm surprised you've heard of Mama Cass, but no. My name's actually Cassiopeia," she said. "My parents had a thing for mythology. I will *not* be naming this little girl after anyone from Greek legends."

Cass stopped in front of a large overhead photo of the complex. "The building is designed a little like a

143

wheel but missing the outer rim. Each wing has the private quarters of one of the owners, but they also hold the offices for the main departments—Programming, Art, Music, and Storyline. Everything blends into the center here."

"I don't know how they keep track of everything," Ahri said.

"It helps that Rafe is brilliant at this stuff."

"And that's not intimidating at all." Ahri blew out a breath. She was good at what she did, but no one had ever called her brilliant. What if she messed up and it looked bad on the company?

"Don't worry." Cass shot her a knowing glance. "He's patient with us mere mortals, and you only have to worry about Rafe. The other guys have their own support staff."

"That's something, I guess."

"But Rafe also carries the biggest burden because he's the CEO. The other guys only have to worry about their departments."

"How are you doing all this alone?" Ahri asked.

"Olaf was the king of organization and worked long hours before he left to set everything up for us. We have a good automation program which helps with the routine stuff. This way."

Ahri followed her into a small cafeteria with tables and chairs in the center. Computer desks with large monitors lined the outside walls. A few had people playing REKD.

"Each floor has a couple of PC cafés," Cass said. "Have you played REKD yet?"

Ahri almost mentioned that she'd played the game since its earliest version but bit back the comment. Cass had given no hint that she knew Ahri's true identity.

"Yes, I play often."

"Good because it's a requirement for employment. Understanding the game is important to every job here."

"That's an interesting approach, but I guess I can see that," Ahri said. "How many people work here?"

"Over a thousand in this location, and there are nearly fifteen hundred worldwide. That's changing, as we open new offices."

"Worldwide?" Ahri felt a twinge of guilt that she didn't already know this about her brother's business.

"We're a global company, with fourteen offices. A new one will be opening this fall in London. They've recruited people for this office from all over the country."

"You don't have a Southern accent. Where do you come from?" Ahri asked.

"All over since I was an Army brat, but I came with my husband. He's one of the musicians and works with Ezreal."

"I don't think Ez likes me." Except for that one sympathetic look, he'd barely acknowledged her, even though he'd been over to Francie's for dinner three times in the last two weeks.

"You've met him already? Don't worry about him; he's a sweetheart. That's just Ezreal's way. He's really shy and stutters when he's nervous." Cass shot Ahri a sidelong glance. "He's especially that way around women he doesn't know. I think he was bullied as a child."

"Kids can be so mean."

"That's probably why he was eventually home schooled." Cass pointed to some plaques on the wall. "One thing that you'll be handling are the charities. The company works with several, but each of the guys has their own endowment set up, and it's Rafe's staff that coordinates and oversees them all."

Kayn had mentioned something about it once. She'd been glad that her brother wasn't blowing all his money on stupid things but was using it to help people—and quietly too. Few people knew how much money he'd donated to charity.

"Something I feel bad about leaving to you is the Midsummer's Eve Event," Cass said.

"I'm guessing it's on Midsummer's Eve." Ahri grinned

"Smart girl. Yes. It's a big cosplay event here at the complex. We've invited the North American pro teams to attend, and there's going to be a banquet that night to honor our biggest fans who've helped to spread the word about the game."

"It sounds like a lot of fun." Ahri took a deep breath. "And a lot of work."

"Right on both accounts. Depending upon when this little lady makes her appearance, I may or may not be able to attend, but I don't live far away. You can always reach me by phone."

"That's a relief." Ahri hoped she hadn't gotten in over her head.

"Anyway, back to the tour. You'll notice a room on each floor that's filled with computers like here in the cafeteria. Three evenings a week you can come in for noob training. There are coaches to help you get better at the game. As I said before, deep understanding of the game really does impact business decisions."

"Okay." All this was way deeper than anything Ahri had ever considered. "I won't need newbie-level help." Her brother had already taught her more than any coach could, she was sure.

"Good. You'll fit right in." Cass shot her an approving glance. "Let's move on."

While a little overwhelmed, Ahri found herself excited by the energy of the place. She thought she'd like working here.

"Well, boss," Cass said as she slipped into a seat across from the conference table when everyone else in the meeting had left. "I think you've got a good one there."

"Glad to hear it." Rafe leaned back in his chair, curious to hear what his assistant thought of Ahri. He fought a twinge of guilt at keeping her identity from Cass because she'd proven herself discreet while working with him. Bill had been emphatic, though. No one besides the guys, the security staff, and Orianna could know Ahri's true identity.

"At first she did look a little intimidated by the size of the organization, but as I introduced her to some key staff, she seemed to get acclimated." Cass gave a soft laugh. "There's no guarantee she won't go home tonight and decide this isn't for her, but I doubt it. You can tell your mother that hers was a good recommendation. I feel confident leaving my responsibilities to Ahri while I'm gone."

"I'll pass it on. You might want to tell her yourself. I think it'd be good for her to hear." Rafe chose his words carefully. "I can't share details, but I know from good sources that she's been through a tough time."

"Then this is the perfect place for her."

"What makes you say that?" Rafe was curious about Cass's input. She'd been there since they'd moved to Boone, coming to work for him after she'd been in another department a few months.

"Because this place has such positive energy. I've never worked anywhere that I've loved this much. How can you beat a place where the employees bring this much enthusiasm to the job? I wasn't a gamer when I started, but I'm hooked now." Cass grinned. "My husband says that's strengthened our marriage."

"Having shared interests is a good thing." Rafe thought about his stepsister, Samantha, Alex's daughter from his first marriage. Sam had married Rafe's roommate. They were such fans of the Magical Realm books that they'd exchanged their vows at the theme park. He powered off his tablet. "I can't imagine marrying somebody who didn't also love this. I've known too many people who didn't have enough to keep them together."

Cass's expression turned reflective. "My mother hated basketball and didn't think my father's obsession with it would be a big deal. That was until basketball season came along, and she became one of those sports widows."

"But I thought you mentioned them celebrating their thirtieth wedding anniversary last month."

"They did. If they had split, I wouldn't have been born. By the end of the basketball season, my mother was ready to leave him. She called home to make sure they'd take her. Grandma told her she could come back, or she could learn to love what he loved."

"Really?" For just a second, Rafe wondered if having common interests would have helped his mother and father's relationship but cast the idea aside. His father's problems had gone far deeper than that.

"Yes. Mom spent the summer reminding herself of why she loved Dad. During her free time, she learned everything she could about basketball. When the next season came around, she was right there beside him on the couch. She got him season tickets for Christmas."

"That's really nice, but it sounds a little one-sided," Rafe said.

"My father was so excited that she'd been willing to do that for him that he got her season tickets to the symphony. She admitted to me that she still doesn't love basketball, but she loves sharing time with my father. He could take or leave the symphony, but he enjoys the time with her." Cass shrugged. "She said it's all about give and take."

"Smart woman. I'll have to keep that in mind if I ever find someone I want to spend my life with." An image of Ahri flitted across his mind, and he pushed it aside. It was much too early for that. He rose, and Cass did too.

"I'm glad to hear you say that. You need a life outside of REKD, Rafe. You never hear of people on their deathbeds wishing they'd spent more time in the office."

"Yeah, yeah. I've gotten that quote before." Rafe turned off the light and pushed back the flush of irritation. He was getting sick and tired of people always telling him that. He and the guys had created something amazing here that engaged millions of people around the world. They had pro players who spent hours, just like Olympic athletes, practicing and honing their skills, who made careers playing his video game. That was a huge life accomplishment.

"But is it enough?" Cass asked, almost as though she could read his mind. She turned and left without another word.

Chapter 10

"Happy Birthday to you," Cass sang as she waddled into the office at the end of the day carrying an oversized muffin from one of the vending machines.

"It's not until tomorrow, but thank you." Ahri gave her a quick hug and took the treat. "How did you find out?"

"A little bird told me." Cass sank into her chair with a sigh. "I'm so glad I'm not expecting in August. Can you imagine how much I'd swell then?" She lifted a foot to showcase her swollen ankle.

"But you'll have a sweet little baby when it's all over," Ahri said, tearing off the cellophane wrapper.

"Hey, I heard it was your birthday," Kristopher Jarvan said as he came into the room.

"Tomorrow," Ahri said with a laugh. "Come and help us eat this."

Kris, Olaf's replacement, took the other seat and accepted a third of the muffin. He seemed like a good kid and had plans to stay in the area after graduation which made Cass happy. Her advancing pregnancy was taking its toll, and Ahri wondered if she'd be able to keep working as long as she planned.

Working for Rafe had turned out to be a bigger challenge than Ahri had expected. He was demanding, and she guessed that came from him being so smart. It really kept her on her toes. When he needed things, he needed them quickly. One good thing was that he wasn't a micromanager. He told her what he needed and then left her to take care of it. It made her stretch, but it also let her be creative in how she fulfilled his requests. So far, he'd approved.

Now, if she just understood how she felt about him. Since those times when she'd been struggling with Zed issues, he hadn't touched her. Every once in a while, she'd catch him watching her with a look that sent a thrill from the top of her head clear down to her toes. But he was always kind and professional, friendly but not too inquisitive. Sometimes she'd hear him chatting with employees as he "managed by walking around." He asked them the same generic questions he'd asked her;

she was nothing special. She had to remind herself that he was her boss, and the best one she'd ever had.

"Do you have any plans for tomorrow?" Cass asked.

"Just a quiet day at home." Ahri would be babysitting Lessa and Nik. When Francie had asked if Ahri could take care of them, she hadn't mentioned it was her birthday. Alex had a weekend conference, and Francie would be going with him. She'd been teaching Ahri to cook, so she could make dinner for the guys on Sunday.

"I mean to have the both of you over to our house for a barbeque once this baby is born, and my body is my own again." Cass arched her ankles again while Kris looked on a little glassy-eyed.

"Don't worry, Kris," Ahri said as she gathered the trash. "She won't go into the girly talk while you're here."

"I can't thank you enough." He rose and brushed off his hands over the wastebasket. "I have two married sisters with kids. When they start in, I leave. Have a good birthday tomorrow, Ahri, and thanks for sharing."

"Thanks." She turned to face Cass. "You sure you shouldn't stop working sooner? I'll bet you can do the rest of your training from home. This *is* a tech company, right?"

"Rafe's already had it set up." Cass slowly got to her feet. "I just don't want to sit at home thinking about how uncomfortable I am. At least here, I'm busy."

"Whatever, but your little lady's going to need her mama to be healthy when she arrives."

"Yes, mother." Cass rolled her eyes.

They walked out of the building together and separated when they reached Cass's car.

Ahri pinched her lips as she approached the giant truck that her brother had lent her to drive. It still amazed her that Kayn had jumped so enthusiastically into the "good old boy" image. Until she'd moved to North Carolina, she hadn't realized the Southern "western" and the one she'd grown up with in Arizona could be different and yet the same.

But seriously, it could have been a mini-monster truck. It still irritated her to have to drive the thing instead of getting a car of her own. When her brother had offered to buy a car for her, Ahri had refused. She wanted to buy one once she could do it under her own name, but Bill had nixed it. He said she had to be patient until they were confident she was safe to assume her true identity.

Ahri had lain awake nights, trying to decide what she would do when she was free again. She loved spending so much time with Kayn. Busy as he was, he always tried to see her every day. Once a week they'd have lunch together and play a game in the PC Café. She hoped no one thought she was dating her brother. That would just be creepy.

And then there was Rafe. Would he be different when she wasn't working for him? Would he be open to seeing her as more than Kayn's sister? Was it too close to Zed's death for her to even be thinking about this?

"Hey, Ahri," a male voice called.

She turned. Ken, one of the artists, was jogging toward her. Rafe had asked her to sit in for him at a couple of meetings about the new champion for which he was writing lore. Ken had sat next to her and been friendly, almost flirting.

"Hey," she said. "What's up?"

"I was wondering if I could take you out to dinner sometime." Ken's words tumbled out, like he was afraid he'd choke on them before he could speak them. It was kind of sweet.

Because of his earlier flirting, she wasn't surprised at the invitation. After living with Francie's family for nearly six weeks, Ahri had come to realize how isolated she and Zed had become, how lonely. She'd been stupid to let that happen, but when she was fretting about Zed, she hadn't been good company for anyone. Or so she'd told herself. Maybe it was time to move on.

"Thank you for the kind invitation," Ahri began, "but I want to be completely open with you. I'm coming off of a breakup."

"So, are you saying no?" Ken asked, his expression an odd mixture of disappointment and wishfulness. "I've enjoyed your company. I want to get to know you better."

"I don't think I'm ready for more than just friends. If that's okay, I'd love to go to dinner with you." His entire countenance lit up which her beat-up self-esteem found flattering.

"Great. When are you free?"

"Not this weekend," she said. "I'll be babysitting for my landlady."

"I could bring dinner to you and keep you company." Ken looked hopeful.

"It's somebody else's kids, so I'm thinking not, but I'd be happy to go out next week sometime. My schedule's open."

"Monday?"

"Sure. Where do you have in mind?"

"Nothing fancy." Ken paused. "Unless you'd like fancy."

"No, simple's fine. I'd like to change my clothes beforehand, so I can meet you there, if that's okay. I prefer to have my own ride."

"Okay. That'll work. I'll text you the location." He pulled out his phone. "What's your number?"

Ahri hesitated. Kayn had added a second phone to his plan for her, but that meant his name showed up as her caller ID. That wouldn't work.

Something niggled at the back of her mind, but it was gone before she could figure out what it was. She'd had no idea that planning a simple date could be so complicated when she was playing incognito. Until she could take back her true identity, she'd have to play it close.

"Send the information to my work email."

"Okay?" His confusion—and she was sure it was hurt—was plain in that single word.

"I can't go into detail, but I had a bad experience earlier this year, so I'm overly cautious now. It's nothing personal," she said.

"I'm not going to go all stalker on you."

"That's good to know." Ahri put a teasing note into her voice. "If I'm too much trouble, I'll understand if you want to back out."

"No. Not at all." Ken's voice came out firm this time, and he sounded more like the man who'd sat beside her in the meetings. "I'll email you."

"Good. I can access my account on my phone, so send it anytime." She pulled out her keys.

"Do you have any food preferences?"

"I like just about everything."

"I'll be in touch then." Ken grinned, backing up. "Have a good weekend." He turned and strode away.

Ahri climbed the steps into Kayn's behemoth. Her first date in years. She hoped wherever Ken chose to go had good parking for this tank. The little worry from earlier returned, and she tried to grasp it. It escaped again. Irritated, she turned the ignition.

Then it hit her. *Kayn's* truck. She'd been blithely driving it between Francie's and the complex. How many people knew he owned the thing? Would they wonder why she was driving his truck? No one had mentioned anything to her. She sent her brother a quick text.

How many people know you own this truck?

Why?

Will anybody connect me with you through it?

Who cares?

Ahri sighed. He was such an idiot sometimes. Maybe she should forward this whole thread to Bill for his take on it.

Do you want people to think I'm your girlfriend?

Gross. Why? Someone talking?

Just answer the question.

I've only driven it once, when I first got it. You're safe.

All right.

She'd better be. As she drove to Francie's, Ahri debated again if she should buy her own little clunker after all. Maybe the Diederiks would help her with it.

When Ahri entered the B&B, she was greeted by the delicious fragrance of freshly baked bread. Her stomach growled.

"I'm home," she called.

"I hope you had a good day." Francie gave Ahri a quick hug when she stepped into the kitchen. "You're off the hook. My weekend guests had a family emergency and canceled, so you and the kids will have the house to yourselves this weekend."

"Okay." Relief washed over Ahri, and she felt a little guilty. Caring for the children was no problem. Stepping in for Francie in the kitchen was a whole other thing.

After the children had taken their baths, Ahri had settled down on the couch to read them a bedtime story. Even though it was a Friday night, Francie had them trained to go to bed early. Car engines and the sound of tires crunching on the gravel driveway made them all perk up.

"It's Rafe's car," Lessa cried as she jumped off the couch.

Nik ran after her, so Ahri followed. What would bring Rafe here tonight? He hadn't mentioned coming over at the office.

Surprisingly, it was Darius who stepped onto the porch first, carrying a box in one hand and a laptop case in the other. Behind him came all four guys, equally laden.

"Hey, Ahri." She opened the door for Darius, and he stepped inside.

"Happy Birthday, sis." Kayn jogged up the steps and kissed her on the cheek. "Since you're babysitting, we decided to bring the party to you."

"Thank you." Still holding the door, she blinked at the burning in her eyes. Of course her brother wouldn't let her ignore her birthday.

As Ezreal brushed past her, he shot her a shy glance and mumbled something that could have been a birthday greeting. Rafe was the last one to the door, Lessa and Nik struggling under the weight of a shopping bag they carried between them.

"I didn't know it's your birthday!" Nik cried, his eyes bright. His birthday had been a few days before she arrived in Boone, so the memory was fresh on his mind. "Rafe brought a cake."

"And Ezreal got the ice cream. See." Lessa tried to lift the bag.

"Show it to her in the kitchen." Rafe grinned at Ahri. "Happy Birthday a little early."

"You all didn't have to do this."

"He fired up his kitchen for the first time and baked you a cake," Kayn said, coming out of the kitchen. "Something called a Hummingbird Cake."

Flushing, Rafe scowled at her brother and made a dismissal sound.

"Kayn said you like bananas." Rafe headed for the kitchen, carrying a square pastry box. "It's got pineapple and pecans too. I hope that's all right."

"It sounds delicious."

Ahri hurried into the kitchen to get down the plates. While Rafe removed the cake from the box, the others made short work of setting up for the party. He used one of his mother's spatulas to straighten the frosting and then sprinkled chopped pecans on top.

"What did you call it again?" she asked.

"Here in the South we call it a Hummingbird Cake," Rafe said. "Rumor has it that it came from Jamaica where it's called a Doctor Bird Cake."

"What kind of frosting?" Ahri asked.

"Cream cheese, of course."

"Can we eat it yet?" Nik whined.

"We have to sing first," Ez whispered. "Remember?"

"What about the candles?" Lessa asked.

"Grownups don't need candles," Ahri said. "Don't remind me of my age."

"Yeah, you're ancient." Kayn pulled out two birthday candles, one in the shape of a two and the other a six, and centered them on the cake. Darius pulled out a lighter and lit them.

Lessa started singing happy birthday, so the others joined in. They ended with Ezreal doing a beautiful harmony. The four guys actually sounded really good together. As Ahri blew out the candles, an idea tickled the back of her mind about having the guys make a quartet for the fall employee party. Would she even still be here?

"Cut the cake," Nik cried. "Cut the cake."

Laughing, she did and then sliced two small pieces for the children.

"It looks like it's mostly fruit," Ahri said, examining her piece.

"Pretty much." Rafe watched her expectantly.

Ahri took a bite and held it in her mouth to let the flavors linger. She hummed softly and smiled.

"I think it's a hit." Darius helped himself to a second piece. "You can make this for my birthday too."

"What's with everyone's laptops?" she asked.

"We're going to have a gaming party," Kayn said, rinsing off his plate.

"Can I play?" Lessa asked.

"Not this time, Lessy-wessy," Rafe said putting the cake, now in its box again, in the refrigerator. "You have time for your bedtime story before getting tucked in."

"But what about presents?" Lessa asked and yawned.

"The four of us are giving her a laptop," Kayn said.

"Really?" Ahri grinned, a little thrill running through her. She'd really missed hers which had been destroyed in the truck fire.

"That's boring," Nik said, his eyelids heavy.

"For you maybe. Let's finish your story and tuck you two into bed." Ahri took their hands, and they climbed the stairs together.

By the time she came downstairs, the guys had the five laptops set up on the kitchen table.

"It's all loaded for you." Kayn tapped on the chair to his left that placed her between him and Rafe.

"Thank you so much, you guys." Ahri ran her hand over the large, sophisticated machine. It was one of the top gaming laptops available, and she knew it must have cost a lot. "There's a community ed class on graphic design that I've wanted to take, and this will be perfect."

"Some would argue that a Mac would be better for graphics," Darius said with a sly grin.

"Yeah. Yeah." Kayn tapped away on his keyboard. "You know it's all in the power of the computer when you're designing. It's not the comp's operating system."

"They'll never let that go," Rafe mumbled on her other side, but the corners of his mouth were turned up.

"Will Alex's internet handle all of us playing at the same time?" Ahri asked.

"That's one thing I insisted they let me upgrade for them since I sometimes babysit Lessa and Nik," Rafe said. "I need a fast, robust connection."

"I call mid lane," Kayn said.

"Jungle, of course," Darius added.

"Bottom lane support," Ahri said, even though she knew none of the others played that role, so there'd be no competition for it.

"Bottom lane carry." Rafe lowered his voice. "Ez is a mean top laner. One of the pro teams offered him a position."

"You're kidding," she whispered, glancing at the quiet musician as he typed away at his keyboard on the opposite end of the table. She'd seen his gameplay a few times but hadn't realized just how good he was.

"Nope. They didn't realize he was an employee and not eligible. That's when we changed all employee's user names to have REKD in front of them to signal to everyone that the user is an employee."

"And I programmed it so if anyone tries to choose a user name with it, the system won't accept it," Kayn said. He'd created a new account for her but must have done some internal tinkering to give her the same level and ranking as her previous one, so she hadn't lost anything with the change.

"How are you going to sign up for that class?" Rafe asked as the game loaded.

"Your mother already has a continuing education account that she's going to let me use. I'm more interested in what I'll learn than getting the certificate of completion."

The game began, and their chatter shifted to it. Once again, she found that she and Rafe worked well together. She knew how to help poke at the opposing champions to bring down their health but then to also support his champs by keeping them alive when they were in a battle.

The evening turned out to be the most fun that Ahri'd had in years. She loved how the guys bantered back and forth, keeping it light enough to make it fun. When they finished their last game, it was nearly midnight.

"Best. Birthday. EVER." Ahri lifted her arms over her head and stretched.

"They didn't believe me," Kayn said, rising. "I taught you well."

She stood and gave him a hug. "Thank you," she whispered and let him go.

He just grinned as he shoved his laptop into its case.

"Let me know if you have any questions on that class," Darius said. "I used to be an art teacher."

"Thanks. I will." She gave him a quick hug.

Ahri stepped back. Out of the corner of her eye, she caught Ez edging around the table like he was afraid she might hug him too. She sat down again so he'd know she wouldn't.

"Thanks for the game, Ez. Rafe. I really appreciate you guys taking the time to do this for me."

Ez mumbled something to Rafe and hurried after Darius who'd gone into the living room to get his jacket.

"What was that about?" she asked Rafe who was taking his time to pack up his equipment.

"He said you were a good player and suggested that we make you a permanent team member."

Ahri blinked. "Wow. Really?"

"I wouldn't lie to you." Rafe grinned. "He commented on that game we played at work and how you meshed well, but that it was only one game. You proved yourself in his eyes tonight. Well done." He pulled a small gift bag from his laptop case and handed it to her. "Just a little something for your birthday."

"You already helped buy my laptop."

"It's just a little something I thought you'd like." He zipped his bag closed and picked it up. "You should have told Ma about your birthday."

"I knew she really wanted to go on this trip with Alex, and she wouldn't have gone if she'd known."

"Well, I'll let you deal with the consequences." Rafe shot her an evil grin and strode from the room.

Ahri gave a soft laugh. She waited until the cars had driven away before she removed the colorful tissue paper from the bag and took out the content. It was a little keychain with her name—spelled correctly—engraved on it. Her heart gave a little hitch that he'd remembered.

R afe had already planned to take Lessa and Nik out on Saturday. When his mother happened to mention that she and Alex were going to a conference for the weekend and leaving Ahri in charge, he'd checked the weather report. It'd be perfect for a little theme park visit. He hadn't been sure about it until Kayn had mentioned it was also her birthday.

Knowing what early risers his brother and sister were, he waited until he thought they'd had breakfast before sending Ahri a text.

Happy Birthday! I forgot to mention that I'd planned to surprise the kids with a trip to Tweetsie today. Would you like to come along?

Rafe tried not to hold his breath as he waited for her response, surprised at his racing heart. What if she'd already made plans with the kids for the day? Maybe he could invite himself along if she had. He was like her big brother, after all.

Tweetsie?

Tweetsie Railroad. It's a Wild West theme park. You know how crazy Nik is about trains.

Sounds like fun. What time?

Is 15 min too soon?

Good thing they finished their jobs. We'll be ready.

At the office, it'd proved a little more difficult than Rafe had expected to keep things strictly professional, at least on his part. He'd found that the more time he spent with Ahri, the more time he *wanted* to spend with her.

He'd risen early and installed the car seats he kept for the kids. The trip would be an innocuous opportunity to be with Ahri in a completely platonic way, all while giving his brother and sister a treat.

Rafe pulled up to the house and, as usual, Nik came running out. From his open window, Rafe heard Ahri call out his mother's warning. His little brother stopped as though tied to an invisible rope that had reached its end. As soon as Rafe put the car in Park, Nik came flying off the porch.

"*Trains.*" The little boy threw himself into Rafe's arms as soon as he was out of the car. "I wanna see trains."

"That's what we're doing. Didn't Ahri tell you?" He tickled the boy until he squealed.

"Can we pet the animals?" Lessa asked from the doorway, her hair pulled back in a French braid.

"Are there animals there?" Ahri asked, locking the front door.

"They have a petting zoo." Rafe found himself staring at her. She wasn't a flirty kind of girl and had a wholesome persona. But then she had those surprising eyes with their sexy tilt that he found so alluring.

"I want to pet a pig." Nik tugged on Rafe's ear.

"We'll do whatever Rafe says is okay." Ahri came down the steps, holding Lessa's hand. "I've never even heard of this place."

"I've gone all the time, ever since I was little," Lessa said proudly.

Rafe bit back a grin, exchanging a glance with Ahri, who was doing the same.

"Yes, I imagine a big girl who's starting first grade in a few months has seen a lot." She said to Rafe, "Your mother left their car seats."

"I have my own." He opened the door, and Nik scrambled in.

"That's convenient." She went to the other side with Lessa and helped with her seatbelt.

"Do you like trains, Ahri?" Nik asked.

"I haven't had a lot to do with them, though I rode one once at Disneyland." It'd been the only time her family had been able to afford to go to the theme park, and they'd had to save for two years to do it.

"Don't you mean Disney *World*?" Lessa asked.

"No, I haven't been to Disney World. I grew up closer to California, so Disneyland is where we went."

"Is that why you talk funny?" Lessa asked.

"That's kind of rude," Rafe said.

"Why? She *does* talk funny."

"I thought you all talked funny," Ahri said.

"See." Lessa's expression turned superior. "It's y'all, not you all."

"I guess I'll have to work on my Southern accent," Ahri said, the corners of her mouth twitching.

"That'd be wise. This *is* God's country, after all." Rafe winked.

"Are we there *yet*?" Nik wailed.

Rafe and Ahri burst out laughing

"I haven't even started the car," he said.

"Then do it." Nik leaned back his head and grunted, "Chugga chugga choo choo."

"Stop it." Lessa slapped his arm, and he began to cry.

"Lessa." Rafe made his tone low and firm, and his sister jerked her head to look at him. "Should we just stay here for the day?"

"No. I'll be good." She poked out her bottom lip.

Nik sniffed and shot his sister a sullen glare. He started with the sounds again, low at first but getting louder.

Ahri looked over her shoulder at him, and he lowered the volume.

"This could be a long day," she said softly to Rafe. "At least at home we can separate them."

"They'll be fine with a little electronic help." He winked and pushed a button to start the movie he'd brought for just that reason. By the time they pulled out of the drive, Nik had forgotten his passive/aggressive taunting of his sister.

"For an only child, you're good with them," Ahri said.

"You are too, for the baby of the family."

Something dark flashed across her face. "I started babysitting when I was ten and did it until I was old enough to get a job to bring in extra money." She stared out her window, the muscles in her jaw working. It reminded him of Kayn whenever he spoke of their father.

"I'm sorry." Rafe had meant it to be some light-hearted teasing, not the start of a heavy discussion. "I know what it's like to have a loser father."

Ahri glanced at him then. "Yes, I think you do." She watched the road ahead for a few seconds before continuing. "We all thought everything was fine. We did okay, I guess. We had what we needed and could usually go on a short vacation every summer. Mom stayed home until I started school, and then she got a job. Then one day Dad didn't come home after work. Instead, he had a friend serve Mom with divorce papers. Just like that, out of nowhere."

"Kayn said if not for you, the two of you would have ended up in foster care."

"I think he exaggerates, but Mom *was* an emotional mess. She still is, to be honest. It's almost like she feels things too much, and it overwhelms her."

"How did they meet?"

"Our father was stationed in Seoul with the Army. One of his buddies was seeing a local girl, and she dragged Mom along. I think it's good she's moved back to Korea. It was hard for her when she came to the US as a bride, but she did it because she loved my father."

"And she stayed because she loved you and Kayn."

"Yeah. She just needed a little help after he left us. I gave her the motivation to get up every morning."

"I wish my father *had* left us." Rafe tightened his grip on the steering wheel as he spoke. "We'd have done just fine financially without him, and it still burns whenever I think about how he treated Ma."

"And you." Ahri glanced at him. "Your mother is one of the loveliest people I've ever met. I'm glad you had her and that she has Alex and the children now."

"Me too." His throat tightened, the last word barely coming out.

"There it is. There it is," Nik cried as he smacked his forehead against the window.

Rafe turned onto Tweetsie Lane and into the parking lot.

"You can't get out of your seat until we're parked, Nik." Ahri reached back and covered the boy's hands.

"*Nik.*" Rafe used his stern voice, and his little brother stopped squirming.

"See how good *I'm* being?" Lessa asked with big-sister arrogance.

Ahri choked back a laugh. "I used to pull that on Kayn."

"Did it work?" Rafe opened his door and jumped out.

"When we were in grade school, but after that he was too cool to care," she said, helping Lessa with her belt. "Let me put on some sunscreen."

His little sister held still, while Ahri sprayed. Rafe had to drag Nik over.

"How about I leave you and Lessa here, and I take this guy back to the house?" Rafe asked.

"No. I'll be good." Nik stood rigidly still so Ahri could spray him.

"You've had two strikes," Rafe said. "One more, and I take you home."

"Okay."

"Thank you, Nik." Ahri brushed aside the boy's hair. "I've never been here, and I'm really looking forward to you showing me everything." He took her hand and started towing her toward the line at the ticket booth.

Lessa slid her hand into Rafe's, and they followed.

"Should we have brought any food?" Ahri asked, scanning the town street filled with gift shops and eateries.

"No, we'll eat here." He stepped beside her. "They have typical theme park food, nothing fancy."

"It's a beautiful location. What's that for?" She pointed to the chairlift.

"Because the park's set on a hill, it can be a nice little hike up to Miner's Mountain," Rafe said. "If it were just the two of us, we could walk it, but we'll take the lift to spare their shorter legs."

"My legs aren't short," Lessa said indignantly.

Rafe came to stand beside her, and he glanced between her legs and his. She giggled.

"Your legs are just the right height for your age," Ahri said. "And Rafe's are perfect for his."

He shot her a curious glance, but she'd looked away. Did he imagine the darkening of her cheeks?

A train whistle broke the silence, and Nik squealed.

"I'm guessing you want to do that first?" Rafe asked.

"Yes. Yes." The boy jumped up and down.

"Lessa wants to go to the petting zoo," Ahri said.

"We'll need to take the lift for that." Rafe took Nik's hand before the boy ran toward the train that was approaching the station. "Let's ride this first."

Lessa heaved out a sigh worthy of a martyr, but she took Ahri's hand without complaining.

As they waited in line, Nik kept up a steady monologue about all his train knowledge and how

Thomas the Train had been there once when his parents had brought him.

"I'll get Nik cleaned up if you'll take care of Lessa," Rafe said, as they carried the drowsy children into the house.

"Good thing we stuffed them there. I'm not sure they'll last long enough to eat dinner."

"Too right," Rafe said.

He took the little boy into one of the guest bathrooms and gave him a quick shower. It was a sign of Nik's fatigue that he didn't complain. He wrapped his arms around Rafe when he carried him to his bedroom.

"Did you have fun today?" Rafe asked as he tucked the bedding over him.

"*Mhm*," Nik mumbled, lifting his arms. Rafe leaned closer, and the little boy planted a fat kiss on his cheek before lying back, his eyelids already closing.

Rafe watched his little brother for a few seconds, his heart full. He picked up the dirty clothes, put them in the hamper, and headed toward the kitchen to check on something for dinner. Passing Lessa's bedroom, he heard her chattering to Ahri.

He checked the fridge first to see if his mother had done the cooking in advance and found a casserole marked as Saturday's dinner. On the counter was a recipe for pork chops with Cheberry Jelly labeled

"Sunday dinner." Ahri had mentioned once that she hadn't done much cooking from scratch and had been learning a lot from Ma. The recipe was pretty straightforward, but he'd love to help her with it. Would Ahri be offended if he offered?

"Oh," Ahri said, putting her hair up as she entered the kitchen, "you've already got it out."

"Looks like Ma set up everything for you." Rafe pointed at the recipe card. "Would you like any company tomorrow while you make that?"

"Are you offering to help?" She looked relieved. "I'll admit I'm nervous to try something on my own especially since you all . . . *y'all* are spoiled by her cooking. I might ruin it."

"Don't worry. Together, we'll make Ma proud." He glanced at the door to the living room as he opened the oven. "Where's Lessa? I thought she'd last a little longer than Nik."

"So did I, until I put her in her nightgown. Once she had it on she climbed into her bed and covered up." Ahri looked a little tired herself, watching him with those delicious eyes. She gave him a soft smile. "You know how to wear out little kids."

Rafe put the casserole dish inside the oven and straightened. "It's not like I have any experience with children. They're a fun pair, and I like living close enough to get to know them. I missed a lot when they were babies, and I was at Harvard."

"Now that you have dinner in the oven, you can help me water the garden." Ahri opened the back door, so Rafe followed her.

"What happened to all that drip system we put in?" he asked.

"That was only for part of it." Ahri pointed to the rear section and the rows of corn. "For some sections, she's still using the irrigation method."

While she fiddled with the controls, Rafe watched Ahri from the corner of his eye. He remembered her saying she was a fast learner, and she was right. Not that he was surprised. She'd picked up her new responsibilities in his office faster than any employee he'd had, even Cass.

He knelt and started pulling weeds. The familiar motion brought back fond memories of his youth and time spent with his mother. The garden had always been a good place to get away from his father.

"We used to have a cow," he said.

"Did you milk it?"

Her teasing eyes and the way the corners of her mouth quirked up made Rafe wonder what it would be like to kiss her. *Down boy.*

"I did, and I know how to make cheese." Rafe puffed out his chest for a second, like it was a huge accomplishment. "We had to make our own cheese because we couldn't afford to buy the store-bought stuff."

Ahri finished with the water. She knelt nearby and started in on the weeds there. "Was it strange for you to go from being a scholarship boy to a billionaire? It was for Kayn."

"Sometimes I still can't get my head around it. My college roommate, Ethan—he's the one who's my brother-in-law now—has an extended family with money, but he was raised on a ranch. I worked there the summer before I started graduate school."

"So, you've been a farmer *and* a rancher?" She shot him an admiring glance.

"Yeah, I have actually. I've been a ranch hand anyway. Funny but I'm prouder of both of those than I am of having a bunch of money. One thing I learned from Jack—that's Ethan's stepfather—was that money doesn't have to change who you are."

"It sounds like that Jack is a wise man."

They worked in silence for a while, until Rafe's muscles started to cramp. He sat back on his heels and arched his back.

"Is that a chicken coop?" She sat back too and pointed to the old hutch.

"Yes. They were too noisy for Alex once they were married. He told Ma that they could afford to buy eggs from the grocery store."

"I'll bet she fought him on it." Ahri stood.

"You're getting to know her. Yes, she did." Rafe rose and brushed off his jeans. "I think she's had trouble adjusting to prosperity too."

"Since you were so poor, when you suddenly had all this money, why didn't you go on a spending spree or take a vacation or something?"

"Partly because we'd already been talking about REKD. To do what we wanted would take capital."

"Kayn bought a condo in Aspen, Colorado, saying he wanted to learn to ski. He only went once."

"He said it was too cold," Rafe said with a chuckle.

"And too quiet, so he sold it. What did you buy when you first got the money?"

"A flashy red Lamborghini." When Ahri stared at him, his face went hot, and he shrugged. "What?"

"I just—" She shook her head. "Sorry."

"No, tell me"

"I've never thought of you as ostentatious."

"That's what Ma called it too. She read me the riot act and told me if I had all that money then I ought to use some of it to make a difference in people's lives. I only kept the car for a year. It drew too much attention, and I didn't like the way it made me feel." He glanced at Ahri. "I donated the money from the sale to the local food bank and listed Ma as the donor."

She gave a little gasp and laughed. "Did she find out?"

"Oh, yeah." Rafe chuckled at the memory. "They sent her a thank you card. She was irritated with me, but I think she liked what I'd done. I did too. That was when I started the charity foundation. I like how I feel about that a whole lot more than a fancy car ever could. I guess a part of me will always be that poor kid who had to work this garden with his mother so they had enough food to eat."

"I think that's a good thing." Ahri lifted her chin, her gaze scanning their surroundings, as she turned in a slow circle.

"What are you thinking?" he asked softly, stepping closer.

"About how peaceful it is here." She glanced at him. "I haven't had peaceful in a very long time." Her eyes glistened, her throat working. She looked down and bent over to pull a weed.

Rafe's heart went out to her. She was sending out those vibes again that she needed to be held. He couldn't be the one to do it, so he shoved his dirty hands in his pockets.

Never in his life had he felt a pull to a woman like this. One way he'd channeled his energy was to start work on a new pair of champions, a brother/sister team. He'd used Ahri and Kayn as his inspiration. Rafe had even started working with one of the artists on the initial concept, and it was hard not to guide the man to make the sister look like Ahri.

"This place is one of the reasons I worked so hard to convince the guys to locate in Boone," he finally said. "Mine was a lonely childhood in a lot of ways. Ma was my biggest champion, and I tried to be hers."

"Did you need to protect her from your father?" Ahri asked, her voice soft.

"Not from anything physical." He felt an adrenaline rush, like he used to get when he'd face off with his father. Evidently Rafe hadn't put that particular monster to rest. He heaved out a deep breath. "He was confined to a wheelchair, so he used words as his weapons. He was a master at tearing us down. That old saying that words can never hurt you is so much sh—" He broke off. "Ma gets mad when I talk like that."

"I understand. Thinking back on it now, it was like that with Zed toward the end. It didn't matter what I said or did. I was wrong." Ahri stared off in the distance, and Rafe wondered what she was seeing in her mind.

"Didn't you have someone you could talk to about it?" Rafe asked.

"No, and that was my fault. I'd always had to protect my mother, so she never had any idea how things really were between us. Kayn never liked Zed, so I couldn't talk to my brother when things went bad. The change was so gradual that I didn't notice it for a long time. I was alone and didn't even realize it."

"No girlfriends?" Rafe couldn't imagine not having anyone to share with.

"By the time I realized how bad things were, I'd drifted away from all but one friend from work. She has a young family and a mother with cancer. I couldn't burden her with my marital problems. When you don't have someone helping you put it in perspective, it's too easy to believe the lies"

"They undermine our self-esteem."

"Yes, but look at what you have now." Ahri studied him, her expression reflective. "Do you ever resent that Nik and Lessa are getting the kind of childhood you'd have liked?"

Rafe considered her words but eventually shook his head. "I'm happy for Ma and grateful she found Alex. He adores her and treats her like the queen she is, and he's crazy about those two kids. I love being part of a large family now. If anything, I think I appreciate Lessa and Nick *more* because I *didn't* have that growing up."

"Someday you'll be a good father," she said, "if you'll make your family as important to you as your business."

He fought an initial flash of anger and took his time choosing his words. "Are you implying that my future family won't come first in my life?"

"I'm saying that's possible if you're not careful. If you're like Kayn—and I think you are—it's something you'll need to decide before you start a family." She took a step forward and kicked at a clod of dirt. "I remember when I realized how *un*important I was to my father. His attorney handled the divorce, and we couldn't afford one of our own. Kayn was in a form of denial. It's sad when a ten-year-old girl is left to figure out how to handle a divorce. Our father got away with paying the least amount in child support that he could. He kept getting behind, and we'd have to threaten to take him to court before he'd pay up."

Ahri heaved out a breath and shook her head. "One time he'd gotten so far behind we thought he'd never pay again. Then suddenly, just like that, he did. All of it. It turns out you can't get a passport if you're behind in child support." She put on an evil grin. "That's one case where I'm glad Big Brother *was* watching. We used the money to get a newer car since our old one was dying."

Rafe stared at her for a few seconds while she looked off in the distance. Why was she sharing this story? He stepped beside her.

"Are you saying you think *I'd* abandon my family?"

Ahri turned to face him, and their gazes met. She reached up and cupped his cheek, her expression gentle, sympathetic. Rafe held still, hurt by her words yet touched by the kindness in her eyes.

"We both know there are different kinds of abandonment," she said, her voice soft. "My father's was physical; your father's was emotional. I don't believe you'd do it on purpose. I'm only saying that as consumed as you are with your business that it's a real possibility. You and my brother both need to consider your priorities when you're ready for a life outside of REKD Gaming."

Ahri started to drop her hand, but Rafe captured it with his and kept it against his cheek. Her touch had sent an electricity through him like he'd never experienced before. Those hazel-green eyes held him, like there was an invisible thread drawing them closer, trying to link them. He craved the tantalizing connection that teased his mind with its almost-touch.

Against his will, held in those mesmerizing eyes of hers, he leaned closer. Ahri must have felt the tug too because she eased in. The pulse in her throat pounded in rhythm with his own. He inhaled and took in her fragrance, a combination of perspiration and her subtle perfume. He wanted to seek it out. Had she put it on behind her ear or on the hollow of her throat?

It was getting hard to breathe. Rafe dropped his gaze to her mouth and found her lips parted, almost an invitation. Was it? He paused, waiting for permission. She edged in. Closing his eyes, he moved close enough to taste her breath.

You're her boss.

With a jolt, Rafe stepped back, stumbling on the uneven ground. He coughed and steadied himself. She stared at him, her cheeks flushing red. His gut wrenched.

His mother's very loud oven timer went off.

"Dinner's ready." Ahri brushed past him and didn't look back.

Rafe shook. He'd blown it. Big time. How could he have given in? Two more months. All he'd had to do was to wait two months, and he hadn't been able to do it. Did she think he'd been teasing her? He clenched and unclenched his hands, letting out slow breaths.

When he was in control again, he returned to the house.

Ahri was pulling out the casserole as he entered, so he washed his hands. The silence weighed on him, but he couldn't make up his mind what to say.

Letting out a slow breath, he took two plates from the cupboard and set them at the table. They needed to have a normal conversation to get past the awkwardness. He had to pretend it hadn't happened, go on as normal. He set the cutlery in place and went to the Frigidaire.

"What would you like to drink with dinner?" He opened it. "There's milk, of *course*, and a couple kinds of juice. You want me to make you some coffee? Ma doesn't drink it, but she keeps some quality instant on hand for her guests who do."

"I don't want anything hot," Ahri said, still not looking at him.

"Oh, look, here's some sweet tea." Rafe pulled out the pitcher and held it up, forcing a smile.

"What is it with you people and sweet tea?" she asked. "Even in the cafe at work, if I want a cup of hot tea, I have to ask for it specifically or they give me iced sweet tea."

"It's a tradition." He put the half-full pitcher on the table, grateful for something normal to talk about. "This, for example, belonged to Granny Gladys's great grandma. It's a family heirloom."

"It's beautiful." Ahri came to the table to examine the pitcher, running her fingers over the delicately painted flowers. "I've meant to ask about it but kept forgetting."

"The family story has it that her husband owned a fleet of ships, and he brought it back for her from one of his cruises." Rafe sat down and signaled for Ahri to do

185

the same. "That was before the War of Northern Aggression."

"The *what?*" Her expression had lightened, and he hoped they were on the way to mending things.

"You northerners call it the Civil War." He scooped out a healthy serving of food onto his plate.

"War of Northern Aggression." Ahri shook her head as she took the spoon he offered and ladled some of the casserole onto her plate. "That certainly wasn't in any of my textbooks."

"Well, the thing is, the side that wins a war gets to write the history books. Not that I'm sorry they won. Funny to think about it though. If the South had won, you'd need a green card to work here." He arched his brows, allowing the corner of his mouth to quirk up. She must have accepted his truce offer because she gave him a half-hearted smile.

At the end of what turned out to be a pleasant meal where they talked about routine stuff they could just as easily have discussed at the office, Rafe rose to clear the table. Ahri's phone went off. She pulled it from her pocket.

"Is it Kayn?" he asked.

"No, it's a work email."

"Who's sending you work emails on a Saturday?"

Her cheeks had gone pink again. That was twice in one day. Rafe stretched so he could see her screen. She caught him and turned away, shooting him a disapproving glare.

His curiosity piqued, Rafe kept trying to catch a glimpse of her phone as he stacked the dishes on the table.

"Will you stop it?" She turned the screen for him to see. "It's from Ken at work. He asked me out for dinner Monday night, and he's telling me where we're going. Satisfied?"

He wasn't satisfied at all. The food in his stomach now felt like a brick. Eight more weeks was a long time if Rafe couldn't be anything to her but her boss while some other guy was hanging around.

"Ken," he said. "You mean Kennen O'Brien in Art?"

Ahri glanced at her phone again. "O'Brien. Yes. I didn't remember his last name."

"You're going out with a guy whose last name you don't even know?" Rafe allowed himself only a slight shake of his head, disapproval coloring his tone.

"What's it to *you* who I go out with?" Her gaze was hard, accusatory.

"It's not," he said. "Does Kayn know?"

"What's with the cross examination?" She didn't quite stamp her foot.

"What if he's with those people who killed Zed?" Rafe snapped his mouth shut, wishing back the words.

Ahri's face had gone white. "It's been weeks, and we've heard nothing. How long am I going to be a prisoner here, hiding away?"

"I'm sorry. I shouldn't have said that. You can go out with whomever you want, but I think it's a good idea to have Bill check out everyone."

"Excuse *me*, but are you suggesting that he wouldn't want to go out with me unless he's a plant, put there by the murderer?"

"I didn't say that, and it's not what I meant. Please, take a breath. I'm an idiot." *On so many levels.*

"You're right."

"What, that Bill should check out anyone you date or that I'm an idiot?"

"Both." Ahri let out a soft laugh, her tense body relaxing. "Let's finish cleaning up. I'm tired."

Rafe decided to only stay long enough to wash the dishes. He'd planned to spend the night in one of the guest rooms, so he could have breakfast with them in the morning, but he was in too emotional a state. He couldn't be sure he could keep control of his mouth. He'd have to wait until the guys came over for dinner.

"Well, I hope you had a nice birthday. I'll call it a day." He dried his hands on the hand towel. "Thanks for coming along. It was fun. I think Lessa especially enjoyed having you there, more so than she'd have had if it'd just been me."

"I think you're wrong there. That little girl adores you."

"I do my best to spoil her."

"There's nothing better for a girl than having a big brother she can idolize."

"From the sister who has a brother she idolizes?" He grinned.

"It was easy with Kayn. Since I was a bit of a geek, having the king of geeks for my big brother was perfect."

"I'm glad you had him." Rafe took a backward step toward the door. "Would you still like some help with dinner tomorrow? I'm not as good a cook as Ma, but I can give you some tips."

She watched him for a second before nodding. "That would take a lot of pressure off me."

"I'll come a couple hours early then."

"All right."

While he drove home, he wondered if he'd ever get to sleep. It was a good thing he didn't have to get up early in the morning because it might be a long night. Maybe he should work on that new champion duo.

When Rafe got home, he flicked on the lights, struck as he'd never been before by the emptiness of his apartment. It practically echoed with it. He thought of his mother's home. That sense of family could be a fragile thing, more so than he'd ever realized before. He wanted to come home every night to a place with that feeling, where the people inside were the most important things in his life.

What Ahri'd said was true. There *were* different kinds of abandonment. Rafe would never want to create a family and then do that to them, but this business was his life. Could he do justice to both?

Ahri had a hard time falling asleep that night. Her mind kept going back to that moment in the garden.

What was it with Francie's garden anyway? First, Rafe had held her there when she'd learned about Zed's murder. Then this afternoon. It'd taken her breath away.

Everything in her life was so messed up. How long could she go on with everything in flux? Would she ever have a chance to go back to her old life?

All this time, and they'd heard nothing about Zed's murder. The Phoenix Police said the leads had gone cold. Enhancing the photo of the person standing by the trees during the funeral hadn't given a clear enough picture to identify anyone.

The man who'd followed her and stolen the truck had an arrest record but only for small-time stuff, like minor drug violations. He hadn't been seen in weeks. Had they found what they wanted in the truck and lost interest in her? Was it safe to return to Phoenix?

Did she want to?

Her thoughts drifted back to Rafe. What was this draw she felt to him? She'd never experienced anything like it. If she let him, he would consume her thoughts. While she'd been emotionally divorced from Zed for a long time, was it too soon after his death for her to get involved with anyone? Was she even ready to start dating? Not that Rafe had asked her out. He couldn't; she worked for him.

Ahri blinked. Was that why he'd stepped back? She was sure he'd been about to kiss her. Well, she'd definitely been about to kiss *him*. She shivered at the memory. How embarrassing if he'd only been acting the nice guy, and she'd misread him. Her body went hot with embarrassment. She was so glad he'd stopped it.

Why was it two in the morning, and she was *still* thinking about him? What was *wrong* with her? Was it because she was lonely? Francie had welcomed Ahri and made her feel at home. She liked her coworkers and got to spend more time with Kayn than she had in years. *Why* was she lonely?

Because everything in her life was temporary right now. She was like a fly on the wall watching other people live. No wonder she craved some kind of connection with someone. Was that why her imagination was making up this thing between her and Rafe?

She forced herself to think of other ways to be part of something. Maybe she should talk to Lessa's piano teacher about helping with those lessons for poor kids.

Ahri was nearly asleep when she heard a sound from down the hall. She slipped out of bed, listening as she went. The moaning came from Lessa's room.

"Don't you feel well?" Ahri asked when she entered Lessa's room, but the only response was a groan. She felt the child's forehead which was too warm. "Where do you hurt, sweetie?"

"My stomach." Lessa groaned again, curling in on herself while she held her abdomen.

"Do you feel like you're going to throw up?"

When the little girl gagged, Ahri raced to the bathroom. She grabbed the trash can and brought it to Lessa. "Use this."

The child moaned but pulled the plastic container to her face. Ahri sat on the bed and patted Lessa's back while she emptied her stomach.

"Why is it doing this?" the child sobbed as another convulsion hit her.

"You probably picked up a bug. Maybe at school."

"Make it stop," Lessa begged between spasms. "*Please.*"

"Poor baby. I wish I could." Ahri's heart broke for the little girl, and she did her best to make her comfortable.

Finally, the convulsions stopped, leaving the child exhausted. Ahri brushed Lessa's hair from her face and pulled the sheet over her shoulders.

"Thank you," the little girl whispered gratefully, her body relaxing into sleep.

Was this the same thing that Rafe had done with Ahri, help someone who was suffering? Did she have some kind of rescuer crush going on because he'd helped her and been nice when her life was falling apart?

The poor man. He'd done something nice, and now she wouldn't let him go. How mortifying. Maybe it was a good thing Ken had asked her out. Mixing with other people more might help her get over this infatuation sooner.

When Ahri thought it was safe, she rose from the bed and washed the trash can. That had been a close call. If she'd woken up even a little later, there would've been a much bigger mess to clean up.

She returned to her room and sent a text to her brother explaining the situation and telling him the guys shouldn't come for dinner. She asked him to let the others know.

It was probably just as well she wouldn't have a cooking lesson with Rafe. It would give her time to put on her office face and then make sure it never fell off again.

Chapter 12

A hri arrived at work Monday morning still a little blurry from the rough night. What a day Sunday had been. Nik had started throwing up in the late afternoon. His parents arrived not long after, so she'd been able to turn his care over to them.

Her new mindset had Ahri looking forward to the date with Ken. There were plenty of reasons she shouldn't think about Rafe as anything other than her boss and one of her brother's best friends. She would *not* make things awkward between any of them.

It helped that Rafe had meetings most of the day, and she hardly saw him. When she did, they were both strictly businesslike, not letting anything personal color their interactions. It was perfect, just how they needed to be around each other.

Then why did it hurt? That was just stupid. She gave herself a mental kick; she *would* get over this rescuer crush.

The next thing she wanted to do was get a status update from Bill. She dropped by his office on the way to lunch and found him sitting at his desk, eating a homemade sandwich.

"What, none of that great food from the cafeteria?" she asked from his doorway.

"My wife enjoys cooking, and she insists on making my lunch. I'm not about to turn down such a gift."

"You're a good man."

"I'm a lucky one." Bill waved her to a seat. "What can I do for you today?"

"I'd like to know if you've heard anything. You know, on my situation." Ahri folded her hands in her lap, trying to calm her nerves. "It's been a few weeks since they stole the truck. How do we know they didn't get what they were looking for? What if I'm hiding in Rafe's office when no one's looking for me anymore—*if* anyone ever was?"

He sat, his eyes slightly narrowed, considering. Was there something he hadn't told her? The acid in her stomach started churning, and she swallowed bile at the back of her throat. How bad were his concerns?

"All I want to know is how long I have to wait before I can be *me* again," she said.

"Aren't you happy here?" He pushed aside his sandwich and did something on his keyboard.

"Yes." Which was correct, but it wasn't the same thing as having her true identity and the freedom to go where she wanted.

"Do you plan to return to Arizona?"

"Maybe." Ahri glanced out his office window. "Maybe not. I haven't decided."

"What's your hurry then? I thought you were working for Rafe while Cass is on maternity leave."

"I am." Why was he making her feel defensive? "But I'd like to know I have a choice when she comes back."

Bill studied her, making her uneasy.

"Please tell me whatever you have." She hated how soft her voice came out. It made her feel weak.

"All right. I wonder if we should call Rafe in here for this."

"He's in an important lunch meeting."

Bill heaved out a breath and leaned forward. "As you know, we've got your decoy, Sona, set up in the New York condo. Her instructions are to act like she's alone in a big unfamiliar city after the murder of her husband, that she believes she's being watched, and she has no friends or family nearby."

Ahri ran her thumb over the badge that hung from her belt, suddenly not feeling sorry for herself anymore. She could be stuck in New York, hiding out. Instead, she was here with family and new friends, working a job she enjoyed. She'd even started helping Lessa's piano teacher with her group lessons for underprivileged kids. Ahri needed to learn to be grateful for what her brother and Rafe, had given her—the semblance of a real life.

"I'd be scared to go out anywhere."

"Exactly," Bill said. "She does leave the penthouse a couple of times a week, but not far, and we have an obvious bodyguard. What we're really watching is someone trying to hack the internet there. Sona has two routers. One is scrambled and rerouted for her personal online use. She's getting a lot of college work done, by the way. The other obvious router has excellent security. It's received several attacks."

"Attacks?" Ahri squeezed the badge in her hand so hard it nearly ripped free. She released it.

"We believe they're trying to hack the system to get access into the apartment."

Ahri leaned forward in her chair, feeling like she might throw up. So they *hadn't* found what they were looking for. What would happen if they managed to break into the penthouse—

She straightened and opened her mouth to speak.

"Don't worry. Sona's safe," Bill said, answering her question before she could ask it. "Remember, it's a penthouse with lots of built-in security already which we've enhanced. We also have paid bodyguards onsite."

Ahri heaved out a breath, not sure she was comforted by that.

"Would you like to know what we've found about your late husband?"

"What?" she asked, her pulse quickening.

"My team found it curious that as soon as one of them initiated a search about Zed Meisner's business accounts, we started getting an unusually high number of hacker hits out of Mexico. We have a private investigator doing some footwork for us in Phoenix."

"I don't understand the significance of Mexico," she said.

"There's the possibility that he was working with some accounts for a company or companies that are fronts for a drug cartel."

Ahri blinked, her mind in a frozen state of disbelief for a few seconds. "This is a bad action movie, right? I'm in a theater, and I can get up and go home."

"I'm sorry." Bill spread his hands in front of him.

She stared at a picture on the wall, not seeing it as her thoughts swirled in different directions. What had Zed been involved with? It'd be nice to be able to tell Bill there was no way her husband would have willingly worked for a drug cartel. The truth was that she didn't know. He'd been a stranger for so long that she wondered if she'd ever really known him.

"It's still preliminary," Bill said.

"Why haven't you told me any of this before?" Ahri couldn't help feeling a little irritated.

"Because we don't have anything conclusive."

"All right." She let out a breath, having to accept his reasoning. "Please let me know if you learn anymore."

"Absolutely."

Bill picked up his sandwich again. Having lost her appetite, Ahri headed for her last training with Cass.

Rafe met the guys for a quick lunch at the PC Café, grateful Ahri wouldn't be there for this first game as an official member of their team. It would give him a chance to casually see what Kayn knew about where Ahri's date was taking her.

"I'm thinking about taking the family out to dinner tonight," he said to Kayn as the game loaded.

"Where to? Ahri's going for pizza." Kayn started tapping the keyboard as the battle began.

"The kids are over their stomach bug and love pizza," Rafe said.

Pizza. He had to play the boss here at the office, but nothing said they couldn't run into each other accidentally. On purpose. He grinned. Nothing would please him more than to see how her date turned out.

"Do you know where your sister's going?" Rafe asked.

"Huh?" Kayn shot him a sidelong glance. "Oh, I think she said Capones."

Ahri drove to the restaurant and found Ken waiting for her at the door. His expression lit up when he saw her. It was the best kind of compliment and just what she needed after that depressing talk with Bill.

"You look really nice," Ken said and signaled the hostess who seated them at a large table.

Ahri glanced around the room, surprised that all the smaller ones were taken up by college-aged couples.

"In the meeting I didn't hear what you do at REKD." Ken said after they'd placed their orders.

"Admin support."

"Ah, a clerk."

"Executive assistant." Ahri decided that while it might be nice if he didn't realize she worked for Rafe, he was bound to find out eventually anyway.

"Oh, up there." Ken looked impressed. "Nice. Did you play REKD before you started to work there?"

"Yes. My older brother is a big gamer, and he got me into it."

"Did he teach you all his secrets?"

"Some." More than anyone would know.

"We ought to meet at lunch sometime and team up."

"That would be fun, but I've been invited to join a team." She searched for another topic, not wanting to say she was on a team with the four owners. "What is it you like about your job?"

That was the perfect question, because Ken turned out to be intensely passionate about his art. He went into lengthy detail about his current project, an update on one of the older champions.

As Ahri listened to him, memories of Zed kept intruding. Once, he'd talked with that kind of enthusiasm. Looking back now, it was easy to see how they'd drifted away from each other. Well, he'd gradually pushed her away, but she'd let him. What surprised her was that her heart didn't ache for the loss of their love. It made her wonder if they'd have lasted anyway. It made her sad.

The server set the pizza down before them.

"I'm sorry." Ken took a piece. "You shouldn't have let me run on like that. I want to know more about you. You don't have a Southern accent, so where are you from?"

She took a bite of her pizza, so she didn't have to answer right away. She hadn't thought about a different history for herself. Thinking back on what Bill had said, she didn't want to say too much, but if she made up a bunch of stuff, she'd have to remember it all.

"We moved around a bit but all out West, you know, Colorado, Arizona, New Mexico."

"Where in New Mexico?" Ken took a sip of his drink. "I have an uncle who lives out there."

"It was when I was really little, so I don't remember a lot about it." Ahri took a big bite of her pizza and said around her food, "Mmm, this is so good."

"Isn't Shen Chinese?" When she nodded, he said, "Your eyes are striking. That's the first thing I noticed about you. I'd love to draw you sometime."

Ahri had gone through this a few times over the years, with white guys fixating on her eyes. If not for the color, she doubted she'd stand out that much. Maybe she should get some brown contacts. Though, he was an artist, so maybe it was only that.

"Thank you, I guess." Then an image of a drawing of her showing up online came to mind. If he mentioned it again, she'd have to come up with an excuse. This hiding was getting really old.

"Do you speak Chinese?"

She was tempted to say something to him in the little Korean she knew because most Americans couldn't tell the difference. She decided against it since so much of the champion mythology came from there. It'd be just her luck that he actually knew some words.

"No. When my mother came from Taiwan, she wanted to be American and only spoke English once she married my father."

"That's a shame. Do you want that last piece?" When Ahri shook her head, he slid it over to his plate. "It's too bad you lost your family's language when immigrating here. Obviously from my last name you know my dad's family came from Ireland. I would have loved to learn Gaelic, but my grandparents had the same attitude as your mom. However," he took on a realistic Irish brogue, "I did learn how to speak English with their accent."

"That's wonderful," Ahri said with a laugh. "Did you ever get to use it in school?"

They lingered at the table sharing high school experiences. He was a lot of fun, but she wasn't attracted to him as more than a friend. She hoped it wouldn't be an issue.

"A table for five," came a familiar voice from the front.

Her heart gave a lurch. What was Rafe doing *here?* She glanced over her shoulder. He stood with his family. Francie hadn't mentioned eating here. It must have been a last-minute thing.

"Ahri!" Lessa skipped over to their table, followed by Nik. They threw their arms around her.

"Hey. I didn't know you were eating out too." Ahri turned to Ken. "They're my . . ." She struggled to think of how to describe them. "My landlord's kids."

"Hello," Ken said. "Which is your favorite pizza?"

They were still trying to tell him, talking over each other, when Francie, Alex, and Rafe joined them.

"I didn't know if you'd still be here." Francie stretched out her hand to Ken. "I'm Francie Diederik. This is my husband, Alex, and our children Nik, Lessa, and Rafe."

Ken gave a gasp and stumbled to his feet. "Mr. Davis." He swallowed and rubbed his hands on his pants.

"Just call me Rafe. Nice to see you again, Ken." Rafe picked up Nik. "I guess my mother introduced my family."

"There's room at our table if you'd like to sit here," Ken offered.

"We wouldn't want to intrude," Francie said at the same time Rafe said, "We'd love to."

There was no way Ahri was going to sit at the table with a guy she'd almost kissed two days ago while she was on a date with another man.

"We've finished eating and need to get going anyway. You're welcome to our table." She stood and said to Nik, "You ought to try the Machine Gun Mike's pizza. I think you'd like it." She grabbed her purse and hugged the children again.

"See you later," Alex said.

Rafe said nothing but watched her with a light furrow between his brows.

Once she and Ken were outside, Ahri took a deep breath. That could have been a disaster.

"Why'd you rush out like that?" Ken asked, disappointed.

"I see enough of Rafe at the office. I don't need to have dinner with him too." Dressed in jeans and a button-down shirt, he'd looked yummy enough to kiss.

"Wait," Ken said, frowning. "Executive assistant. You work for Mr. Davis?"

"He said to call him Rafe, but yes."

"I thought his assistant was pregnant."

"I'm filling in until she gets back from maternity leave."

"Oh, man. We could've had dinner with the CEO of REKD." Ken glanced wistfully at the restaurant. "I have some ideas I'd love to present to him."

"Really? You want to intrude on his family time so you can pitch work ideas to him?" Ahri shook her head. "You can bring any ideas up to him at the office. He's good at that kind of thing."

"I wasn't in a hurry to end our evening, either." His ears turned pink.

"The weather's nice this evening," Ahri said, trying to shift the topic away from Rafe. She glanced up the street. "Do you want to do some window shopping?"

"Sure."

They spent the next half hour strolling the lane looking at the shops. By the time they'd returned to the restaurant, it was getting chilly, and Ahri was ready to get home.

"Thank you for a fun evening." Through the window, she saw Rafe glance her way. Their gazes met, and she felt that draw to him again. Seriously, it was getting ridiculous.

"I hope you'll let me take you out again." Ken stepped a little closer and broke her connection.

If Ahri hadn't been caught up with Rafe, she'd have realized Ken's intent. As it was, he was already leaning in to kiss her before she did. She managed to turn her face at the last minute, and he kissed her cheek instead. His ears went red again.

"Friends, remember." She gave his cheek a quick peck and forced herself not to look toward the restaurant.

"Right," Ken said, sounding disappointed. "Sorry."

"I had fun. Thank you." Ahri turned and headed for Kayn's behemoth truck.

"I reckon work must be wearing you down," Rafe's mother said to him when Alex took Nik to the restroom.

"Why?" Rafe continued to stare at Ahri and her date outside the restaurant. Was Ken going to kiss her? He *was*. Something primal seemed to flow from Rafe's chest up into his skull, blurring the edges of his vision. Ahri turned her head at the last minute, and he wanted to whoop.

"Because you seem a little preoccupied tonight," his mother said, her tone droll.

Rafe shifted his gaze and found her watching him, looking very much like she wanted to laugh. At him. He straightened, clearing his throat.

"You like her," she said.

"Like who?" Lessa looked up from the paper she was coloring.

"Ahri," Ma said.

"Oh, I like her. She's so nice." His little sister pointed to a crayon near him. "I can't reach the green."

"I like her too." Rafe handed it to her and met his mother's gaze. "Too much since I'm her boss."

His mother did laugh then. "That was our problem too."

"Yes, but you were able to transfer to another professor in the same department." He pulled out his phone. "Transferring her would be a demotion, and I need her there until Cass comes back."

"Then be her friend for now." Ma reached over and covered his hand with hers.

"And what if she falls for someone in the meantime?"

"Just make sure that someone is *you*." She winked.

Rafe had never thought of his mother as devious before.

Chapter 13

"Hey, Ma." Rafe stepped through the kitchen's back door the following Saturday.

He was proud of himself for playing it cool and professional all week. However, he'd helped weed the garden three evenings and enjoyed partnering with Ahri during a game with the guys at the PC Café at lunch.

"To what do we owe this honor?" his mother asked, amusement coloring her voice as she shot a sidelong glance at Ahri where she sat chopping vegetables.

"When I was here the other day, Lessa mentioned she wanted to go mining."

"To Foggy Mountain?" His mother frowned. "She just went there with her class a month ago."

"Is that where she got those stones she carries around all the time?" Ahri asked.

"Yes," Francie said.

"She wants more of them for a bracelet." Rafe shrugged. "I told her once she had enough that I'd have them set for her. Is she here?"

"She is. I'll get her," his mother said. "Do you want to take Nik too?"

"If he wants to come." Rafe forced himself not to look at Ahri, but from the movement in the corner of his eyes, he reckoned she'd looked up at him.

"He'll go anywhere with you," his mother said with a laugh. "I'll get them. They're upstairs pretending to do their chores."

Rafe wandered over to the table where Ahri was working. "Need any help with that?"

"I'm just finishing." She started scooping the cut vegetables into a bowl. "Are you taking them to a real mine?"

"Not underground, if that's what you mean." He took the seat across from her. "Foggy Mountain has buckets of ore that people buy and then pan the contents for gems."

Ahri paused, her hands over the bowl. "You mean like panning for gold?"

"Essentially."

"It's sweet of you to do that for her. Lessa talks about gems a lot. She even checked out a book on them from the library."

"She showed it to me," Rafe said. "That's what gave me the idea."

Feet pounding down the stairs made him turn to the door. Lessa burst through and flung herself into his arms.

"Are you really taking me to get my gems?" she asked breathlessly.

"If you want to come," he teased.

"Yes, yes!" She started jumping up and down.

"Good luck if she's this excited already." Ahri stood and picked up the bowl.

Nik came running into the room squealing, his arms waving in the air. She glanced at Rafe, trying not to laugh. He kept his own grin to himself. She'd be coming along, even if she didn't know it yet.

"Calm down, Nik, or I'm not taking you anywhere," Rafe said, and his little brother let out a martyred sigh.

"Off to the mines, I hear," Alex said, entering the kitchen and tickling his children. "You two be good for Rafe. He's a busy man and doesn't have to do these nice things for you."

"I wanna mine for gold," Nik said.

Lessa let out a disgusted sound. "We're going *gem* mining. They only have fool's gold."

"What's fool's gold?" Nik asked, temporarily distracted.

"It looks like you're in for it today, Rafe." Alex sent him a sympathetic grin.

"Yes, sir, I am."

Lessa grabbed his hand and started tugging him toward the living room, so Nik took his other and joined in. Once there, Rafe pulled them to a stop.

"Do you think there's anyone else in the house who'd like to go gem mining?" he asked his little sister, whose gaze immediately darted to the kitchen.

"Can Ahri come with us?" she asked.

"Why don't you invite her?" After Lessa ran back to the kitchen and started begging Ahri to come, he squatted down, taking his time to tie Nik's shoe which had conveniently come undone.

At the office, Rafe had overheard her confirm that she had another date planned with Ken. Rafe might not be able to date her, but that didn't mean he couldn't find ways to spend plenty of time with her.

It hadn't taken very long after he'd made that decision that his old doubts had returned in force. Why did Tess's final words have to be the ones he couldn't shake? *You were never enough. You'll never be enough.*

"Ow. Not so tight," Nik whined.

"Sorry." Rafe loosened the laces. "That better?"

"I guess I'm going with you to the mine," Ahri said hesitantly from the kitchen doorway. "I hope you don't mind."

"Not at all." Rafe stood. "I'll buckle these two in their seats while you get your things."

"I'll be right out."

He focused his attention on the thought that it was Ahri he'd be spending the morning with and not bad memories.

Lessa spent the beginning of the drive chatting away about the different gems she hoped to mine. Ahri seemed a little preoccupied and never glanced at Rafe once. The atmosphere had the feel of a delicate negotiation, and every move had the potential to blow up in his face. If they hadn't had several moments of connection like that one in the garden, he might have thought she wasn't interested in him. He had to hold on to that thought.

"You're really quiet today," he said to Ahri when Lessa ran out of things to say. "Did you do anything fun last night?"

"I helped Lessa's piano teacher with her group lesson," Ahri said, still not looking at him.

Rafe waited for her to say more, but she didn't. This was supposed to be a chance for them to get to know each other better, but how could they if she didn't engage in a discussion?

"Did you like it?"

"The kids are cute, but there are too many of them for just two of us. I'll be glad when Ezreal has time to help."

"He can ask around his team for more helpers."

Ahri nodded but said nothing more. He needed to get her to smile and searched his mind for a humorous topic. At the memory of her turning her face away from Ken, the corner of Rafe's mouth twitched.

"What's the most embarrassing thing that's ever happened to you on a date?" he asked.

She shot him a considering look. "I'll only share if you do."

"All right. I'll even lead off." Rafe chuckled at the memory. "I was a freshman at Harvard and was taking out this girl from one of my classes. I was so nervous I forgot my wallet and didn't realize until the waiter brought the bill. She said she'd pay, but they wouldn't take her card. I called my roommate Ethan to bring mine, but he was in a theater on a date of his own."

"What did you do?" Ahri had straightened, finally showing some interest.

"She had to call her roommate to bring another card." After all that time, his face still heated up thinking about it.

"You couldn't have called your mother to get her number?"

"That was before Ma married Alex, and finances were too tight." Rafe shook his head. "Better to suffer that humiliation than hit her up for money she didn't have."

Ahri watched him for a few seconds before looking away. "You're a good son."

"I try to be the kind of son she deserves." He coughed at a sudden tightness in his throat. Self-conscious, he said, "It's your turn."

"Okay," she said. "A friend of mine in high school had this really cute stepbrother that I'd been crushing on. I can't remember the details, but they were having a party at their house, and I was invited—as his *special* guest. I thought I'd hit the jackpot. I took special care with how I looked and everything. I hadn't been there very long when she confided in me that he was interested in another girl at the party, and she wanted to set them up."

"Ouch. Nice friend."

"Yeah. I thought I'd misunderstood the invitation. I only stayed for a little while. He'd been really nice to me and even walked me to the door. Nice manners for a host, I thought, but when he acted like he wanted to kiss me, I went brain dead and backed away."

"Oh no," Rafe said, understanding. "*He'd* thought it was a date too?"

"Yep." Ahri let out a deep sigh. "My friend asked me the next day what I'd been playing at. *She* was mad at *me* for treating her brother like that."

"A date that wasn't a date but was. Do you think she set you up?" he asked.

"No. She wasn't that kind of girl. I've always preferred to think she was just a little dense about how inappropriate it was for her to talk to me about that if I was supposed to be his date. I kept hoping he'd ask me out again, but it never happened. My friend got her way. He and that girl became an item a couple of weeks later." Ahri glanced at him. "It's funny. I haven't thought about that in years."

"Sorry it was a bad memory."

"It *is* funny now, looking back. I was just sensitive then and was going through a tough time, and it fit my fatalistic attitude." She gave a rueful laugh. "Upon reflection, I seem to have had a lot of tough times."

"I'm sorry." Rafe reached over and clasped her hand. He'd meant it to comfort her. She shot him a quick glance with those amazing eyes of hers. A shudder went through her, and she laced their fingers, color flooding her cheeks.

Ahri had misunderstood Rafe's gesture. He should pull back his hand. Except hers felt so good, so *right* in his that he didn't want to. Besides, after her story, he didn't want her to feel rejected by him too.

Fortunately, they'd reached the mine, and he needed both hands. When he'd parked, he took charge of Nik, while Ahri helped Lessa from the car.

"I'll get the tickets and a bucket." He strode ahead, leaving her with the children, so he could collect his thoughts. If he didn't handle this right, she might think him rude.

What should he do? His supposedly brilliant mind betrayed him, only leaving him with the remembered sensation of holding her hand. *Holding her hand.* What was he, twelve again? His mother was right that he needed a life if something as simple as holding a woman's hand could mess with his head so thoroughly.

"We're ready," Rafe said when he had everything.

"What?" Lessa stood with her feet planted, hands on her waist. "Only *one?*"

"We don't need two." He frowned at her. "Nik's more interested in the rocks than the gems anyway."

"The buckets aren't cheap," Ahri said. "You should be grateful that he's doing this for you."

"But he has *lots* of money."

Ahri faced her, mimicking Lessa's posture. "And it's *his* money. He doesn't *have* to spend a penny of it on spoiled little girls who don't appreciate his gift. You better be careful, or he may stop giving you nice things."

Rafe wanted to grin at Ahri's defense of him. Lessa looked about to argue but, as he'd seen happen numerous times, her defiance seemed to crumble and her bottom lip began to tremble.

"I'm sorry," she said with glistening eyes.

He was about to tell her it wasn't a problem, but Ahri held up a hand to stop him.

"What else?" she asked.

Lessa's lip turned pouty.

"This is the same thing we talked about when Mrs. Fortune changed the time of your piano lesson." Ahri watched his sister expectantly.

"Thank you?" His sister looked so pathetic that Rafe picked her up and hugged her.

Ahri leaned in to kiss Lessa's cheek, and her hair tickled Rafe's neck and the smell of her perfume filled his senses. *Get a grip, man.*

"It's all right, Lessy-wessy," Rafe said. "You know how long it takes to sift through the stones. I think this bucket will be fine for us."

He put her down, took her hand, and picked up the bucket with his other one. They found a place in front of the water trough that had room for the four of them to work together. He set it up so the bucket sat between Ahri and him, with the children on each of their sides.

Rafe started by putting two scoops of ore into Ahri's strainer box.

"Once you rinse these"—he demonstrated by setting the box into the water and sliding it back and forth—"you'll be looking for anything clear, colored, or black. When you can't find anymore, you dump these in the bucket on the ground."

"I know." Lessa pulled the box closer to her and started picking through it.

"But Ahri doesn't," he said.

"Some of these are quite pretty." Ahri picked up a colorful rock. "It's not a gem, but I like it."

Rafe helped Nik with their batch, pulling out the gems Lessa would want to look at.

"What's something you've always wanted to do?" He had to lean in close so he could be heard over the sound of the equipment.

"What do you mean?"

"If you could do anything you wanted, go anywhere, where would it be?"

Ahri's expression turned contemplative. "I've always been pretty practical. Except for a single trip to Korea before my father left, we didn't do a lot of traveling. We took one vacation to California when Kayn graduated from high school. I always knew I couldn't afford to go anywhere, so I didn't waste time dreaming about things that could never happen."

"I understand that since I was too poor to pay attention."

"*What?*" she asked, laughing.

"It's just an expression. Even now, the only traveling I've done outside of the US has been for the company."

"Really? Even though you can afford to travel, you don't?" She shot him a sidelong glance.

"Not yet, though I've been thinking a lot about what Ma said. I do need to have more fun. Lately, I've been thinking about making a Bucket List of places I'd like to visit. I've asked the guys for suggestions, and they're even more boring than I am."

"Kayn, especially." Ahri shook her head. "Give him a dark room and a computer with good Internet, and he's in heaven. Zed's death has brought home how much I've missed. He wasn't even thirty."

She looked so sad that her body language cried out with a need to be held. Rafe tightened his grip on the box to keep from pulling her into his arms. He needed to distract her.

"Let's create a Bucket List then," he said.

"But will you actually go anywhere on yours?" she asked.

"Sure, when things have settled down at work."

"I think that's part of your problem." She eyed him.

"What do you mean?"

"All four of you guys are waiting for things to settle down before you start *living*. Don't you understand yet that life will never settle down?"

Rafe paused. "I'll have to think about that."

"You said you were looking to do something fun. Do you have anything in mind that you can add to *your* Bucket List?" Ahri asked.

"My brother-in-law Ethan has an interesting family," Rafe said. "He has a brother who went on a cruise and ended up stranded on a Pacific island for over two years. I think I'd enjoy a cruise, as long as I didn't get shipwrecked."

"Getting shipwrecked would definitely not be on my Bucket List either. It's not very likely anyway." Ahri grinned. "I think a cruise would be fun, but I wouldn't want to go if I got seasick."

"I think they have medicine now to help with that. I've never seen you carsick."

"I don't get carsick."

"Then I'll bet you won't get seasick either."

"Where would your cruise go?"

"I like the fall colors," he said, thinking through the options he'd looked up. "There are cruises that go up and down the Eastern seaboard between Florida and Canada. That might be fun."

"They have some singles cruises." Ahri scooped more ore for Lessa. "I had a coworker in Arizona who used to go on those. She saved all her vacation time for them. I can't see that kind of trip for myself. I'm afraid they'd be full of expectations for hooking up." She shuddered. "That's just not me. But I have always thought it'd be fun to take a river cruise."

"Along the Mississippi River?"

"No, in Europe. If I were to confess to having a Bucket List, I guess a river cruise would be my dream trip. I've wanted to visit Europe, but I hate the idea of hauling luggage around from hotel to hotel. On a ship, you get to sleep in the same bed every night." Her expression turned a little dreamy. "I'm okay having the ship's itinerary planned for me. When I'm on vacation, I don't want to have to think about too much. It'd be different if I knew somebody who lived in the cities I was visiting who could take me to places the normal tourists don't go. It's never been anything I could afford, so it's a pipe dream anyway."

A European river cruise. That actually sounded intriguing to Rafe. He knew what he was going to check out when he got home.

DONNA K. WEAVER

Chapter 14

"She's beautiful, Cass." Ahri accepted the little bundle and inhaled the sweet, freshly-bathed baby smell. She glanced around the pretty little backyard where Cass's husband Jax was chatting with Rafe's other assistant, Kris, by the grill. "It's nice of you to have us over."

"Oh, we love doing this kind of thing. Jax has already had two barbecues for his coworkers since the baby was born. When it's his party, I make him do all the work." She grinned. "With my mother gone back home, I needed to be around some people again."

"It must be hard having your mother so far away."

"I love having her—for *short* visits. She's a bit of a control freak and can be too much of a good thing." Cass gave a dark chuckle, her tone going sarcastic. "Funny, but in my own home I kind of think *I* should be the boss, so you can imagine the tug-of-wars we have. Jax spends a lot of time in his workshop when she's visiting."

"I can't imagine it." Ahri's mother had always been happy letting someone else be in charge. Ahri would never have to worry about 'who's the boss wars' when she ever remarried and started a family. *If* she did.

"How's the Midsummer's Eve event coming?" Cass studied her. "You haven't called to ask as many questions the last couple of weeks."

"No, your early suggestions really helped. I think I'm getting the hang of how Rafe likes things. I'm so glad he's not a micromanager. I had one of those on my first job, and he killed all my desire to do well." She shook her head in disgust at the memory. It hadn't been long before she'd been job hunting again after that experience.

"How are you settling in outside of work?" Cass asked.

"I'm almost finished with my graphic design class." Ahri's excitement had raised her volume, and the baby stirred. She lowered her voice. "I've been dabbling at book cover design. My instructor said I have a knack for it."

"Kris said something about you dragging him to a food kitchen?"

"He has a gift for exaggeration, that one," Ahri said. "It's a food pantry, and he helped me stock shelves with donations from local grocery stores one afternoon. You know, dented cans and stuff they can't sell but is still edible."

"He told me he enjoyed it and signed up to help again." Cass glanced over at the guys, a small curve to her mouth. "He's from a well-to-do family, and I think it was an eye-opening experience for him."

Ahri didn't mention that Bill had been uncomfortable with it and had insisted on doing a background search on everyone on the payroll. He'd only agreed to her going the one time and had only allowed her to work in the back. Since the hacking attempts on the security of the New York penthouse had continued, he thought the transient nature of the place would make it easier for someone who was looking for her to go unnoticed.

He hadn't said it outright, but that made Ahri think he was worried they might not only be focusing on New York. That had given her a sleepless night which made her angry that these people she didn't even know could control her life without even being there. She was determined to live as normal a life as possible.

"Are you making friends?" Cass asked, pulling Ahri from her thoughts. Cass arched a brow and gave her a *tell me all, girl* look. "Are you dating anyone?"

"I've been out a couple of times with groups, once with people from work and another with the members of my community ed class. And, yes," Ahri said before her friend could press, "I've been on a couple of dates, but I'm not looking for a boyfriend."

How could she tell her that the high point of her life came on Friday nights when she played REKD with the guys? She'd learned not to schedule a Friday night date for that very reason. They took turns hosting at their apartments and supplying the treats. Ezreal still wouldn't talk to her except during a game, but he did occasionally look at her. Darius had provided some great feedback on her graphics class project too.

"So you're settling in."

"I am." It surprised Ahri how quickly she'd come to feel at home in this place and with these people, much more so than she had in recent years in Arizona. She and Taliyah were drifting apart. She was expecting again— her last one, she insisted—and pregnancy never agreed with her. It made her sick and cranky. Their last phone call had been a little terse. Ahri might have to wait until after the baby was born to talk to her friend more.

"How many children do you think you'll have?" Ahri asked, and Cass laughed.

"That's probably not the best thing to ask a woman who just gave birth a few weeks ago and whose newborn just slept through the night for the first time." She sighed. "Six solid hours. When I woke this morning, I thought I'd died and gone to heaven. I'm such a boring person now, appreciating simple things like sleep."

"They're so much work, such a responsibility." Ahri brushed aside a curl of dark hair from the baby's forehead.

"I never dreamed I'd feel this way." Cass's eyes shone. "My mother used to tell me that a baby was proof that your heart could live outside of your body, and I thought she was exaggerating. Now I completely understand."

As Ahri drove home later after promising to come again, she thought about her friend's words. Cass could say things like that from the safety of a loving, secure relationship. How could Ahri ever find one if she couldn't get over her fixation with Rafe?

Ahri had been thinking about that when she drove to work on Monday. It was still on her mind during a rare lull at the office when she glanced out her window and saw Kayn outside. His outdoor meeting had just ended and his team scattered, but he continued to sit on a bench by himself.

"I'm taking a break, Kris."

"I'll be here," he said without looking up from his work.

Ahri made her way to her brother and sat beside him.

"Hey." He took one look at her face and closed his laptop. "You look like you need to talk. Want to go to my apartment?"

"This should be fine."

"What's bothering you? Zed?"

"Am I that obvious?" She rubbed her forehead.

"You've been through a lot." Kayn shot her a sympathetic glance.

"It's so much more than that. I feel like I'm making progress but . . ."

"But what?"

"I used to think I was a good judge of character."

"You know I never liked Zed. I thought he was too much into money and status, but I honestly thought you'd help him get over that since you're not."

"How much has Bill told you?" she asked.

"Everything he's told you. I know they've had to up security at the penthouse several times."

"Not that." She straightened, not wanting to think of Sona sitting there playing the decoy.

"About the money laundering?"

"Yeah."

"I can believe it. Zed told me once when you two first started dating that he was going to make it big. He had *plans.*" Kayn snorted in disgust. "More than anything, he wanted to impress his family."

"I remember those dreams. I kept telling him that those weren't things I was interested in. I thought he'd given up on them." Ahri gave a soft, disgusted *huh.* "My confidence is trashed. How can I ever trust myself to believe in someone again?"

"You sound like Rafe now."

"What do you mean?" She tried not to sound too interested.

"He used to date a lot, even had a couple of girlfriends during college. Nothing really serious. Until he met Tess." It was Kayn's turn to sound disgusted. "None of us liked her, including his roommate Ethan. But Rafe was so *into* her."

"Like I was with Zed?"

"Exactly, and she didn't like us any better than we liked her. We realized pretty soon that if we said anything against her that he'd drop us—friends he'd had for *years.*"

Ahri sighed in sympathy. She'd once told Kayn that if he said one more bad thing against Zed that she'd delete her brother's phone number. Guilt flooded her that he'd gone through that with two people.

"I'm sorry I was a brat about Zed."

Kayn patted her back. "The school of hard knocks can be brutal."

"Too right."

"In the end, it was Zed who chose his path. You had no control of that."

She accepted the truth in her brother's statement.

"What happened with Tess?" she asked.

"She waited to dump him until he proposed."

Ahri felt sick to her stomach. For everything that Zed might have messed up, she believed he'd loved her. At least in the beginning.

"It happened not long before our sale went public. Like with you, it totally ruined his self-confidence. He hasn't dated anyone since."

Something in the tone of Kayn's voice made her peer at him more closely. He was watching her, the corner of his mouth quirking up. What else did he know? She recalled that time in the garden when she'd been sure Rafe was about to kiss her. The memory made her heart thud hard, and she had to force her breath to slow down.

If she was right and her brother thought Rafe was interested in her, then she wasn't imagining it. The thought almost made her smile.

Chapter 15

"Rafe seems to enjoy spending time with the kids."
Ahri bent to pull a weed, trying to sound casual,
while her nerves threatened to overload in
anticipation. Where he used to come only occasionally
on a Saturday, the last few weeks he'd come every week.

"Yes." Francie wore one of her gentle smiles as she
glanced at Ahri from the corner of her eye. "I think some
of it's because Rafe always wanted to be part of a larger
family."

"He mentioned something about that to me. He said
it's why he pushed the guys so hard to headquarter the
business here." Ahri used the top of her gloved hand to
wipe her brow.

"It wasn't easy, either," Francie said. "The Boone council is tight on growth and what the boys were proposing was huge for this area. If Rafe hadn't wanted it so badly, they might have convinced him to give up on it. I think what finally sold the council was the number and quality of high-paying jobs the business could offer. I don't understand how economies work, but I do know that we're now considered a tech city. I think that's what Alex called it anyway."

"Yes. I've read that. A lot of other tech companies have shown an interest in locating here."

Maybe Ahri should broaden her job search to some of those companies instead of just looking at the university's job list. She only had two more weeks before Cass returned.

"Thank you so much for all the hard work you do here," Francie said when they'd finished. She straightened and arched her back.

"I'm the one who should be thanking you." Ahri pulled off her gloves. "I wish you'd let me pay rent."

"You're like family, and I don't charge family for staying here. Besides, you earn your keep." At the sound of an engine, Francie turned toward the house. "That must be Alex."

"What are you going to do with a Saturday just to yourselves?" Ahri asked, following her inside.

"Rafe's the one who arranged the play day. He said he's got something planned with us." Francie continued into the living room to meet her husband.

What was Rafe doing that didn't include the kids? Ahri tried not to think about it too much. The man confused her so much. When he'd taken her hand back at the gem mine, she'd thought it had meant something. It hadn't, and she'd felt like a fool afterward. Having her brother hint there might be more to Rafe's feelings for her had kept her awake for a few nights. She'd let it go when his behavior toward her had been strictly businesslike. Ahri was the one who was trying to make it more than it was.

As for his adventure today, she might not be invited, and she thought that would probably be for the best. He or the kids had invited her on every one so far, and she'd loved it. If her life had to be on hold, she couldn't think of a better person to pass the time with than Rafe. And his family, of course. Just friends.

With the upgrade launch completed and an incredible success, he'd had a lot more free time and had been spending it at his mother's house. He might as well live there. That thought drove home how much she'd miss him when she wasn't working for him anymore. What would she do when he wasn't such a fixture in her life?

Ahri sat at the kitchen table and opened her laptop. Instead of going to the university's page, she did a general search for employment in Boone. When her job ended, she had to have some way to support herself. She wouldn't freeload off her brother.

She'd only read a few job descriptions, when she heard the familiar sound of Rafe's SUV. Her pulse went insane as it always did whenever she heard it. Ahri stayed at the table, not wanting to make it obvious to the world how much she craved to see him, even though it'd only been about ten hours since she'd spent the evening supporting his champion in their weekly game nights.

After a few minutes, Francie hurried into the kitchen, followed by Alex and Rafe. A faint sheen of perspiration dotted her normally calm face, and she wrung her hands.

"Is everything all right?" Ahri jumped to her feet, alarmed until she saw Rafe's cheeky grin.

"Have you ever gone zip lining?" Francie asked, a little breathless.

"Nope." Ahri sat back down, trying to hide her disappointment.

"Rafe and Alex want me to go with them," Francie said, her voice pleading.

Ahri looked up again. Did her landlady need help telling the guys she didn't want to go? Ahri glanced from Alex to Rafe, who both watched her expectantly.

"Um . . ."

"They really want me to try it out, but I don't want to be the only one there who hasn't done it before." Francie took the seat next to Ahri's. "Will you come too, so I don't look like a fool?"

"I don't like the sensation of falling." Ahri's heart thudded so hard it hurt at the thought, even as she felt guilty for the lame excuse. The Diederiks had done so much for her, Francie especially.

"It doesn't feel like you're falling," Alex said.

"It's like you're flying. It's amazing." Rafe's expression now resembled his mother's pleading one—minus the abject terror.

"It'll feel like I'm about to *die*." Ahri held up her pointer finger when they started to argue. "You two stay out of this." She turned to Francie and asked softly. "Are you sure you want to do this?"

"If I follow the rules, I'll be right as rain. I've wanted to do this since Rafe told me about his first time. We couldn't afford to do anything like this when he was in high school. I'm not getting any younger, and I don't want Lessa and Nik to have a cowardly old woman for their mother."

"There's nothing cowardly about you." Ahri rubbed the spot over her heart. Finally, she let out a long breath and said to Rafe, "If I die, tell Kayn to send my Korean doll to my mother."

He let out a whoop and pulled her into a hug. Ahri stilled, her cheek pressed against his shoulder, his aftershave—now one of her favorite smells—filling her senses. Time seemed to suspend, and she wanted to stay there forever. Someone coughed.

Rafe released her. He stepped back and put his hands in his pockets. "Y'all need to put on some solid, closed-toe shoes." He lifted a foot to show his hiking boots.

Still a little unsettled by the hug, Ahri heaved a sigh and met her hostess's gaze. "I guess we're going ziplining."

Grinning, they left the room.

"Don't even say it," Rafe said to Alex when he could hear the women's footsteps on the stairs. "I didn't mean to do it."

"You've been walking a fine line, and you may have just crossed it." Alex leaned against the counter, one leg crossed in front of the other.

"I know." Rafe started pacing the kitchen. "Like I said; I didn't mean to do it. It's hard."

"Maybe you should take a business trip and get away from her for a few days, or you could just not come over here every dang day. I sympathize, but any man would be tempted if he spent so much time with a woman he cared about."

Rafe paused and rubbed his face. "Maybe I will. It wouldn't hurt to do a surprise visit to the London facility."

"Have you told her how you feel?"

"That wouldn't be awkward at all, would it?" Rafe had considered it, but they still had to work together for a couple more weeks. Her responses made him think she was at least attracted to him. He'd taken his mother's advice and thought they were good friends now. Rafe wanted more but did Ahri?

"I made the mistake of not talking to your mother and almost ruined it for us before it'd really begun." Alex gently clasped Rafe's shoulder.

"What if I'm already too invested in her, and she leaves?" Rafe asked, his voice soft.

"Everything worth having comes with a risk." Alex grinned. "How invested *are* you?"

"I'm not going to say I'm in love with her, but I've never felt this strongly about anyone before." Not even Tess. That realization and speaking aloud the thoughts Rafe had been having brought a surprising release. His shoulders relaxed.

"Then I'd say she's worth taking your time. You want to do it right."

"Where are we going?" Ahri asked when they were on the road.

"It's a place called Sky Valley," Rafe said.

"It's in Blowing Rock." Alex rubbed his wife's neck.

"Oh, that's where Tweetsie's at," Ahri said. "And those cute shops."

"Yep," Rafe said. "And don't forget that hike we took."

"I've been trying to talk Francie into doing this since we got married," Alex said. "The young'uns need to be at least ten before they can come with us, but I reckoned it'd would be good for her to get her feet wet before then."

"You sure don't want Ma to scare them to death," Rafe chuckled.

"You behave yourself," Francie said, giving him a mock glare, "or I'm going to jerk a knot in your tail."

"You're in trouble now." Ahri laughed, loving their fun banter.

When they arrived, Rafe led them to another small group that was gathering. The staff were expecting them and passed out their harnesses and helmets. While the guides were assisting the others, Alex worked with Francie and Rafe helped Ahri into hers.

"Hey, you talked her into coming," Kayn called, jogging up to them, followed by Ezreal and Darius.

"You knew about this?" Ahri shot her brother an accusatory glare, but he only grinned.

"Of course we did. We do this every year, a couple times." He gave her a one-armed hug. "I'll admit I didn't think you'd agree to come along."

"It seems she'll do anything for Ma," Rafe said.

"Hey, Mrs. D." Kayn gave Francie a hug.

"Now you boys will all see what a big coward I am," she said.

"Piece of cake," Darius said. "I've been ziplining all over the world. This one's nice and easy for a start."

They joked about other trips they'd made, even Ezreal, as they got into their harnesses and helmets. It was nice to see how normal he could act when he wasn't talking to her.

"Looks like you've done this before," one of the guides said as he checked Ahri's harness.

"No, but he has." She pointed to Rafe.

Everyone loaded into some jeeps and began what turned out to be a drive up some rough terrain.

"I thought we'd be closer," she said, bouncing in her seat.

"They'll do a safety briefing first." Rafe steadied her. "They have to get us up so we can zip down."

Once there, a guide went over their instructions. Ahri tried to review the things he said. What if she forgot something important?

"I don't know if I can remember all of this," Francie whispered.

"I was thinking the same thing," Ahri agreed.

"There will be guides at every platform, so don't worry." Alex put an arm around his wife's shoulders which seemed to buoy up her courage.

"What if I get up on one of those platforms and then find I can't do it?" Ahri held her arms to her stomach.

"You'll do fine." Rafe rubbed her back the same way he did Lessa's when trying to comfort her. "You're braver than you give yourself credit for."

"They don't just hook you up and send you on your way," Alex said. "You'll get a chance to practice first."

"And I can control how fast I go, right?" Francie asked.

"Yes," Alex said.

"Just don't brake too much so you get stuck short of the platform," Rafe added.

"*What?*" Ahri stared at him, her mouth dry. Grinning, Rafe gave her chin at gentle nudge. "Don't worry if you do." He shoved his hands in his pockets again. "It happens all the time, and y'all will have your harnesses on. It's easy enough to tow yourself to the platform. Now, Ma, don't look at me like that. Would Alex let you do this if he thought you'd get hurt?"

"Well, no." Francie glanced at her husband.

"It's just a matter of learning how much to brake to keep from going too fast but not braking too much." Alex gave her an encouraging nod.

"Have you been working out?" Rafe asked Ahri. "I know Ma lifts weights with Alex a couple times a week."

"Yes. Why?"

Rafe lifted up his right arm and tightened his bicep. Ahri stared at him, her eyes wide, fighting to keep a neutral expression. He seemed to realize what he'd done and dropped his arm with a cough.

"If you've been lifting weights," he said, "you'll hurt less tomorrow, both arms and hands."

"Oh." Ahri had to resist the impulse to fan herself. "I guess I'm glad I didn't already do my workout this morning."

The short test run looked like a child's version of the longer zip lines and reminded her of the shorter, simpler water slides in Phoenix. Once she'd done one, she'd felt enough of a rush that she'd have been happy doing those instead and could only hope the zip line would be the same.

"Can we stay here and just do these?" Francie asked.

"Brilliant minds think alike," Ahri said with a laugh.

"No, Ma." Rafe didn't quite roll his eyes, and Ahri gave him a soft jab in the ribs.

"The first lines are the easiest ones, so you can get used to them," Alex said.

"The first time could be the last time," Francie said, wringing her hands again.

Alex pulled his wife into his arms and held her, whispering. Not wanting to intrude, Ahri turned and found Rafe watching her.

"You sure you're okay to do this?" he asked. "I think you'll enjoy it, but I probably shouldn't have pressured you."

"I won't let Francie down." Ahri took a deep breath and exhaled slowly.

"That's my girl." Rafe reached over and ran his knuckles down her cheek in a gentle caress. Her breath caught, and she found herself leaning into his hand. He held it there for a second longer before dropping it and putting his hands back in his pockets.

"So, is this going to be like going down the bunny slope when skiing?" Ahri asked. Not that she'd ever been. That might be something else to look forward to, skiing in the Blue Ridge Mountains.

"I guess. Hadn't really thought about it," Rafe said. "Looks like we're next."

Rafe watched over Ahri while his stepfather kept an eye on Ma. Alex had worked on her for weeks to convince her to come along this year. His mother wanting to include Ahri had been the frosting on the cake as far as Rafe was concerned.

Ahri. That girl got under his skin like no woman he'd known. He hadn't had such a fun summer in years. Too often he caught himself wanting to take her hand. He'd found it safer to keep his hands in his pockets, so he didn't forget himself. Now, if he'd just remember to keep them there.

After his stepfather's comment, Rafe had been haunted by the big question of whether or not she was nice to him only because he was her boss. Alex was right. Rafe needed to make himself scarce for a while.

The ugly little voice in his head whispered that she was only putting up with him because she needed the job, that if she had a choice it wouldn't be him. Over the years, he'd had several girlfriends, though none of the breakups had scarred him the way the one with Tess had.

Maybe he'd have gotten past it better if his life hadn't turned upside down with the change in his fortune a few weeks later. At least when he'd dated in high school and college he'd known they wanted him for himself, in spite of being the poor kid. Suddenly he was the face of the Billionaire Boys, and women were throwing themselves at him. Or at his money.

Ahri wasn't like them. She had a billionaire brother and had refused to take money from him. Rafe needed to stop the self-doubt and enjoy this time with her.

"You ready for this?" he whispered to Ahri.

"Am I ready to leap to my death, you mean?" She did look a little green.

Rafe chuckled. She could give Lessa a run for the crown of martyr queen.

"How shall we do this?" he asked the group.

"Well, *I'm* sure not going first," Ahri said.

"I will," Alex said. "Then Francie."

"Okay." His mother took a deep breath, and Alex put his arm around her again. He glanced at Rafe and Ahri.

"I'll go after Ahri," Rafe said.

"Why?" Ahri looked up at him. "So you can listen to me scream all the way down?"

"Do you scream on roller coasters?"

"Yeah. Why? It's part of the fun."

"Then scream to your heart's content on this. I did— just like a baby the first time I went."

"Did you really?" Ahri grinned, a mischievous twinkle in her eyes. She glanced to where her brother and the other guys were waiting.

"Yes, and they all know it since they were there so don't think you can use it against me." Rafe pointed to the launch station. "There goes Alex."

She let out a little moan and stepped beside his mother. Rafe watched as they clung together. He loved the way Ahri and Ma looked out for each other.

Then it was his mother's turn. He moved beside Ahri and together they offered comforting platitudes. Ma let out one initial scream and then went silent. Hopefully, it was a good sign.

"You ready?" he asked softly.

Ahri looked up at him, her eyes terrified and her hands shaking. "Promise me I won't die."

"You won't die."

"Lighten up and just enjoy the ride," Kayn said in his most condescending big-brother tone from behind.

Ahri seemed to steel herself and stepped to the mark. She put her hands on the brake over her head, listening to last-minute instructions from the guide. Then she was off.

Her scream was as much frightened as it was a thrilled whoop. She made him proud with her northern equivalent to a Rebel Yell. He'd make her into a Southerner yet.

"I didn't think you'd get her to do that," Kayn said.

"Nah. It wasn't me." Rafe looked at his friend. "It was Ma."

"Now we'll see if she'll ever do it again."

"Next," the guide said.

Rafe stepped up and took the familiar position. When it was time, he heaved out a breath and launched himself from the platform, embracing the thrill. As he sailed over the canopy of bright green forest, he listened for the rustling of the trees over the sound of the zip line. He wondered if Ahri had been able to hear it with all her screaming.

She waited for him on the platform, almost dancing with anticipation as he approached. He landed easily, and the guide unhooked him from the zip line and reconnected him to the tree wire.

"You didn't die," he said.

Ahri threw her arms around his waist, and he embraced her. She trembled, but he didn't know if it was from excitement or residual adrenaline.

"I thought I was going to a couple of times." She looked up at him. "It was epic and one of the most frightening things ever." She blinked, seeming to realize what she'd done. Her cheeks colored, and she moved to step back. He didn't want to let her go but did.

"Now just six more to go," he said.

Ahri groaned.

Chapter 16

"Only a few more days and you'll be back here full time." Ahri snuggled Cass's infant. Every time she saw her, the baby seemed to have grown even more. "I don't know how you can leave her behind."

"Didn't you know?" Cass asked, scanning through the final plans for the Midsummers Eve Cosplay event. "Rafe's letting me do up that little office as a nursery."

No one *had* mentioned that to Ahri, but she shouldn't have been surprised that he'd agreed to do something like that. They already had an in-house daycare center. He and the guys spent a lot of time making REKD Gaming a good place to work. When her brother had talked about his part in the business, she hadn't paid that much attention.

However, since working here, she'd been reading articles about the company online and was impressed, especially since they had such good employee candidates. REKD was listed as one of the best companies to work for, and lots of talented people vied for positions with them. It came as no surprise that Rafe had made sure his assistant, who faced leaving behind her first child, had someplace for the baby until she was big enough to go to the daycare.

Ahri's rescuer crush hadn't eased off at all since that first incredible moment in the garden. If anything, it'd gotten stronger. The more time she spent with Rafe, the harder she was falling. He'd been gone more than a week, and she couldn't believe how much she missed him.

Sunday's dinner hadn't been the same, and the weekday evenings felt flat without him there to play board games, or garden, or go hiking with. Since he'd been gone, the guys hadn't had their Friday game night. He'd return on Thursday, and the big event was Saturday.

And then she wouldn't work here anymore.

Rafe had become such a good friend. Her *best* friend, if she was honest. She hadn't had one of those in a very long time. Before he'd left, his behavior had confused her, touching her tenderly one moment and then pulling back. She'd caught him watching her a few times. If she'd seen that look on the face of a man she was dating, she'd know he wanted to kiss her. But she wasn't dating Rafe.

"You seem a little preoccupied." Cass left her chair to stand by Ahri and said in the high-pitched voice adults tended to use with babies, "Is my little precious distracting you?"

"Not exactly." It did drive home to Ahri how unsettled her life still was, and she was sick of it.

"What's troubling you then?"

"I'm not sure where I'm going when you return."

The baby started to fuss, and Cass took her back. "I think you should stay right here in Boone."

"I've been checking for positions at the university." Ahri went to stand by the window with a view over the REKD campus. She recognized most of the faces now.

"Why not take another job at REKD?" Cass, rocking the baby in her arms, came to stand beside her.

"The competition is fierce, and there aren't that many openings."

"Before I left, Rafe and I were discussing the possibility of hiring a third assistant. You've done a great job." Cass kissed the baby's forehead. "You should apply."

"I don't want to work for Rafe." Ahri's whole body flushed with frustration that threatened to burst from her.

"Hasn't he been nice—" Cass blinked. "*Oh.*"

Ahri turned from the window.

"It's like that, is it?" Cass's expression had clouded. "That's unfortunate. Do you know how he feels about you?"

"I don't *know*." Ahri words came out too loud. She started pacing, fighting the words that wanted to explode from her. Cass watched her sympathetically. Over the weeks, she'd become a dear friend. Ahri let out a deep breath. "Sometimes when he looks at me . . . it takes my breath away. What if I'm imagining it because I *want* it to be real?"

"What if you're *not* imagining it?" Cass pointed to the chair she'd been sitting in before. "Sit down." She put the baby in her carrier and took the desk chair. "You're staying at his mother's house. Do you ever see him away from the office?"

"Until he left on this trip, I saw him almost every day." Ahri crossed her arms over her stomach, as though that would calm the butterfly dance festival going on in there. "After the launch, he's come after work to help with the garden. On Saturdays he takes the kids somewhere, and they always invite me to come along. We've been hiking and biking and mining. We went on a zip line tour. I thought I was going to die, by the way. His parents came on that one."

"It sounds like a wonderful summer so far. I've been here since almost the beginning, and I'm going to be honest with you. Rafe loves his family, and he's really attentive. But he's never been *that* involved." Cass grinned. "I don't think you're imagining it."

Ahri held her stomach tighter, afraid she might throw up.

"Well, I need to get this little one home before she wants to eat again." Cass leaned over and squeezed Ahri's hand. "He's needed someone to draw him away from work. I'm glad to hear this."

"Glad to hear what?" Rafe asked, striding into the office. He looked delicious in his blue jeans and REKD T-shirt. His normally well-styled hair had a mussed look to it, as though he'd been running his hands through it.

Ahri's heart leapt into her throat, and she shot a panicked look at Cass who merely returned an encouraging smile.

"Nice to see you, Cass," he said to his assistant, though he continued to look at Ahri. "You look better." He came over to the carrier and squatted down.

Cass grinned, her eyes wide as she nodded to Ahri and mouthed *You've got this.*

"Go ahead and pick her up," Cass said to Rafe.

He gently slid his hand underneath the infant and lifted her. For a second, his gaze met Ahri's again. That draw to him spiked, followed by something warm and luscious. She recognized it as a fulfilling sense of peace, and she had to remind herself that he was her boss.

As she watched him coo at the baby, bouncing her as he tried to tease a smile from her, Ahri's heart twisted. Someday, when he married, he'd hold his own baby like that. A powerful longing to share that with him hit her. With it came something she hadn't felt in weeks: fear. She'd thought she and Zed would share a family and look where that had led.

Her father hadn't wanted her. Zed hadn't wanted her. Why should she think that Rafe did? Cass hadn't been here all these weeks and had simply said what Ahri wanted to hear. There was no basis for it. He was her boss, her friend. Nothing more. The thought sat in her throat like a rock.

The baby started to fuss, and he handed her to Cass. While they talked, Ahri wondered what she was going to do when she didn't see Rafe all the time. She had to find another job soon. She didn't want to be so far away from her brother again. Maybe she could find work in Charlotte. It was a larger city but still close enough to see Kayn frequently.

Between the federal government and the Phoenix Police Department, the case of Zed's murder was at a standstill. After her talk with Kayn about Zed, she'd wondered more and more if her late husband had known what he was involved with. If he'd been seeking money, she could imagine him convincing himself that helping a drug cartel to launder money would be an easy way to get it. But what could he possibly have that they wanted so badly? She'd been in such a hurry when she'd packed that she hadn't looked at their things closely. Now it was too late.

She thought back to the promising jobs that had just opened up, one at the university and one with a local tech company. At some point, she'd get her life back. Ahri's gaze met Rafe's, a soft smile pulling at his lips. It made her heart thump hard. Yes, she would especially miss him.

"Ahri has everything ready for Saturday," Cass said. "I'm planning to drop by."

"In costume?" Rafe asked.

"Of course." Cass picked up the baby carrier. "I just wish I had the figure now to wear the one I wanted. None of your champions has a matronly look about them."

"I know." Rafe heaved out a breath. "Ahri's always giving Darius and his artists a hard time about their clothing choices for our female champions."

"And lack of armor," Ahri couldn't help adding.

"Well, now that I've had a baby, I feel sorry for a couple of your lady champs." Cass patted her chest above her large bosom. "If those women were real and ever had a baby, they wouldn't be able to hold themselves upright."

Ahri burst out laughing, and Rafe gave a grudging and embarrassed chuckle.

"It's a *fantasy* game," he said.

"That's what you always say. Bye." Cass waved as she left, and Ahri returned to the desk.

"What am I going to do with you two?" Rafe asked as he headed to his office.

Chapter 17

F or the next two days, Rafe hardly had a moment to talk with Ahri about anything except work. If he hadn't been exhausted when he fell into bed at night, he doubted he'd have been able to sleep. He couldn't wait for Saturday night when he could finally talk to her.

The team Cass had assembled and then Ahri worked with had done an impressive job, especially for an almost last-minute event. He'd originally thought to open it to the public without charging. Bill, with Ahri and Cass to back him up, had nixed that. Instead, they'd charged enough for general admission to help offset the cost of the food. It made it expensive enough to discourage potential party crashers but not so much that it would keep dedicated fans from attending.

Dressed in a tux, Rafe headed to the balcony that overlooked the main grounds where the partygoers had gathered. Kayn, Ezreal, and Darius waited for him just inside, also dressed like their favorite champions.

"Seriously? That's your cosplay costume? A *tux*?" Kayn asked, dressed in sleeveless armor, baggy pants, and boots, his curved blade hanging at his side.

"I chose the skin from the Debonair line. I'm still armed." Rafe held up the over-sized hexed technology rifle his champion used. It even had a blade, though that had been made of a soft, bendable material. The mock-up of the magical gun was still relatively heavy, in spite of having been made of lightweight materials. It was a real work of art. He'd ordered a case built for it so it could be displayed in the building's entry after the event.

"You play him a lot, so it fits." Ez held up his hands to indicate his own flashy swashbuckler jacket and pirate-like pants, his champion's powerful gauntlet held in his right hand.

"It works." Darius had gone with his champion's default gear of armor, cape, and a giant ax.

"Yeah, but he already had the tux, so he didn't have to do anything." Kayn shook his head. "Except for his gun, he looks like he's going to prom."

"In here," Ahri said as she opened the door, dressed in the full armor of one of their support champs, from a helmet on her head down to a breastplate and even the cuisse that covered her thighs. Rafe knew it wasn't one she liked to play, but she approved of how much coverage it provided. She shot him a quick glance, taking in his costume, and the corner of her mouth quirked appreciatively.

Behind her, a crowd of young men and one woman entered the room, all dressed as REKD champs.

"Our pro teams have arrived. Welcome." Rafe strode over and shook everyone's hands, nodding especially to the ones he'd played against in Phoenix. "I'm so glad you could all make it. Your fans out there will go insane when I announce you."

"It's time." Ahri pointed to a clock on the wall.

"Okay. I'll give my opening comments," Rafe explained to the teams, "and then I'll introduce you. You're welcome to mix and mingle with our guests after that. There are food and craft vendors and some costume contests. Tonight, at the private banquet, we'll have a table for each team, including the fans who've won the chance to eat with you." He grinned and pointed to the balcony. "We're on."

He led the way, followed by his partners. They stood beside him at the handrail, the members of the pro teams behind them.

"REKD. REKD," the fans below chanted.

"This is surreal," Kayn muttered.

"Tell me about it," one of the team members said from behind them. "It still blows my mind."

"Is the game really your initials?" another team member asked.

"Rafe, Ezreal, Kayn, and Darius. Aren't they just so clever?" Ahri's voice dripped with sarcasm.

"That's just because every time I play against you, you get wrecked," Kayn sniped back.

Grinning at the sibling rivalry, Rafe picked up the microphone, holding up his other hand for the crowd to quiet. When they did, he began.

"Welcome everyone to REKD Gaming and what could be our first annual Midsummer's Eve Celebration."

The crowd roared, and a rush of excitement filled him. All these people stood as proof that he and the guys had created something that had captured the imagination of millions of people.

"Thank you for coming to our little party. Tonight, at our banquet, we'll be handing out awards honoring our most dedicated players who've done so much to spread the word about REKD and to encourage others to join our game. It's because of their diligence and devotion that we've grown so much so fast."

It took a while for the crowd to calm down.

"You're in for a treat this afternoon. Let me now introduce our *special* guests."

Rafe introduced each team, letting the crowd vent their enthusiasm before moving on to the next one. He then invited everyone to enjoy the day.

Turning, he faced the teams. "Thank you again for coming today. I hope you enjoyed your tour of the facility last night. Have fun."

Aware that Ahri wasn't moving, Rafe held back as the others left. He'd been waiting for a chance to get her alone. When the room had emptied, he turned to her.

"I've hardly seen you since I got back." He slowly approached her.

"Do you need something?" She glanced at his hand, that he'd been tapping, and he stilled it.

"I need a lot of things." Rafe was so nervous he couldn't quite look at her.

"How can I help?"

Rafe swallowed and shifted his shoulders. He would do it, declare his feelings for her. But what if she wasn't interested?

"Have you heard something from Bill?" she asked.

He blinked, confused. "No, why?"

"Because you seem . . . nervous?" she asked, hesitant.

"You read me like no one I know." Rafe looked up to heaven, pleading for help. He heaved out a breath and glanced at her again. "I'm just going to say it and get it off my chest and hope that you don't take it wrong."

Ahri's complexion paled.

"I'm really attracted to you, and I want to take you out when you don't work for me anymore." Rafe said the words in a rush. "There, I said it." He felt a little sick and had to force himself not to tense up, the memory of Tess's rejection echoing in the back of his mind.

Ahri stared at him for a few seconds, her expression inscrutable.

"Do you mean like a date?" she finally asked, the words airy, like she couldn't breathe. Was he imagining the hopefulness in her voice?

"Exactly that." The tenseness in Rafe eased, and he grinned. "More than one date. *Lots* of dates. I should have said something to you sooner, but I didn't want to make things awkward between us here. So, I ran away to London instead."

Ahri grinned back at him. They stood staring at each other stupidly.

"I'd like that." She reached up as though to touch his face but started to drop it.

"Don't." Rafe captured her hand and pressed it against his chest. He tried to cup her face with his other hand but was blocked by her armor. "Why did you wear all this?"

"Because a true warrior maiden isn't going into battle dressed in lingerie." Ahri scowled at him through her visor.

"I *love* this about you, but the helmet's got to go." He removed it and tossed it aside.

"Hey. Be careful with that."

"I'll be careful with *this*." Rafe cupped her face in his hands, his heart full and his pulse nearly deafening him. "I've wanted to do this for a *very* long time."

He slowly lowered his face to hers, watching her beautiful eyes to make sure she knew his intent and had time to pull back if she wanted to. She didn't, instead closing her eyes as she lifted her chin. He touched his mouth to hers, slowly to savor the feel of her warm, soft lips.

His heart swelled like to burst from his chest, and he deepened the kiss. He wanted to hold her, taste her. Rafe moved his hands around her clunky armor. Ahri responded by pressing into him. Something sharp stabbed into his chest.

"Ow." He stepped back and rubbed his right pec.

"Oops. Sorry." Laughing softly, Ahri ran her fingers over the spot. "I hope it didn't break the skin."

"I'll find out later." Rafe took her hands in his and kissed her again.

"Well, I guess that answers that question," came Cass's familiar voice behind him.

Rafe spun around, keeping himself a little in front of Ahri, his neck turning dark. "It's the first time I've kissed her, and she won't be working for me tomorrow."

"Then I won't report it to Orianna," Cass said, mockingly stern.

Ahri moved fully beside him, and he asked, "What question is answered?"

"If you felt the same way she does." Cass grinned.

Rafe glanced down at Ahri, wondering what the two women had discussed about it. She shrugged.

"I really do need her though," Cass said

"Wait, I didn't get to ask you," he said when Ahri stepped toward his assistant.

"What?"

"Will you sit with me at the banquet?"

"I'd love to." Her gaze darted to his mouth, but she pressed her lips together, her cheeks flushing.

"Do you have a dress here?" Rafe asked. "*Don't* wear the armor."

Ahri laughed and hurried away with Cass. He stood for a few seconds, enjoying the incredible way he felt, like he'd just finished the best zip line ride of his life. Thinking ahead to when she'd be his partner at the banquet, he wondered what she'd wear. It'd better not be that armor because he really did want to hold her properly.

Still grinning, Rafe picked up his clunky rifle, settled it on his shoulder, and headed out to the party.

Chapter 18

A
hri had run from one responsibility to another all day, her emotions soaring. Heavens. That *kiss.* She'd pinched herself several times to make sure she wasn't dreaming. If she weren't so tired, she'd dance.

The Midsummer's Eve event had been a huge success. She was glad she'd been able to talk Cass into adding food and craft vendors along with the face painting. It'd added a carnival-like atmosphere. Ahri had loved watching the families, parents and children geeking out together in costume.

As security guards escorted the last of the day visitors out, Ahri headed inside the building. It was a good thing she'd spent the last couple of nights in Kayn's apartment. The only cocktail dress she owned was there.

She'd planned to wear her armor to the banquet, but Rafe's comment had her second guessing her decision. She didn't want to wear anything that would keep her from getting more kisses. All she had to do was change and freshen up, and then she'd meet Rafe.

Giddiness filled her again. She was going to the banquet with *him*. With his simple statement—and those amazing kisses—he'd blown away all her doubts.

Ahri used her employee fob to enter the building. The empty lobby had an eerie feel to it, and she slowed her stride. Busy work places always seemed creepy to her whenever she'd had to come in after hours. This was the first time she'd experienced that here. Since it was a worldwide company, the place had always seemed to be full of teams working on projects around the clock.

Before, she'd always entered Kayn's apartment through his private entrance. As she approached the programming wing door, she stopped. It stood ajar.

Her brother was a creature of habit, and he *always* locked his doors. It was something they'd both picked up after living in poor areas in Arizona. Francie was always teasing Ahri about locking the front door when they were all home, but she did it automatically. Kayn was the same way.

Could he have been in such a hurry today that he'd forgotten? Her gut told her he wouldn't. Maybe someone from his programming team had needed something in one of the conference rooms and left it open.

Maybe not. Ahri groaned. Maybe she was making something out of nothing. No one but an employee could get inside anyway. Right?

Should she send her brother a text about it as a precaution? Maybe someone on his team *had* come in the building for something—and hadn't noticed that one of the guests had gotten in behind them? A prankster could do a lot of damage. She pinched her lips, torn between calling security and checking it out herself. If she raised an alarm and it was nothing, she'd look stupid.

The hair stood up on the back of her neck; she wasn't alone.

"Now here's my favorite lady in armor," Rafe's voice came from behind her.

Ahri let out a breath. She turned around. He looked a little worn from the busy day but still yummy. Putting one finger to her lips, she pointed with her other hand at the open door. Frowning, he darted to her side and pulled her back a few steps.

"It's not Kayn?" he whispered.

"I don't think so." She pulled out her phone and sent her brother a quick text about the door. "Should you call one of the security guards?"

"I'm tempted," Rafe said, still staring at the door, "but if it turns out to be nothing, I'd hate to have dragged one of them away from rounding up any straggling guests outside. That could be an even bigger issue. I can see that next year we'll have to assign someone to inside duty."

"How would somebody get inside anyway?" she asked.

"That, my love, is the $60 million question."

Ahri warmed at the endearment, in spite of her worry about that open door. She rewarded him with a quick kiss.

When Rafe hefted his toy weapon onto his shoulder as though preparing to go into battle, she lifted her shield in front of them. At least her armor was really made of metal and would offer some protection if there were a problem.

He eased the door open the rest of the way with his foot. They edged into the hallway, the only lights from those in the floorboards on each side and the exit sign. There was no glow under the conference room doors where Kayn's programming group held their meetings. Ahri tiptoed closer to the door that accessed her brother's apartment. It also stood ajar.

"No way would he have missed closing *two* doors," she whispered, taking out her phone and texting Kayn another message.

Intruder in your apt.

"Agreed," Rafe said softly, pulling her back a step. "I think we'll wait for reinforcements."

What was with him, grabbing her like she couldn't take care of herself? It was kind of sweet, him playing the protector, even if it irritated her a little.

266

"I think you should keep going forward," a gravelly voice said from behind them.

At the same time Rafe spun around, Ahri turned, holding up her shield as a barrier. She hadn't recognized the man's voice, but she did his face. The earring she'd told the police about glittered in the emergency exit lighting to the side. He must have been out among their guests because he wore the remnants of a lame costume.

"It's *him*," she breathed.

"Yes, Mrs. Meisner. It's me." His droll tone still had an edge to it. He nodded toward Rafe. "Do you really plan to *shoot* me with that?"

"No, but I might hit you with it." Rafe raised his rifle like a bat.

"Only if you want to die right away." The man lifted his hand from his side to show a revolver.

With a gasp, Ahri held her shield higher, so angry that her hand shook. This man was tied to Zed's murder, might have even been the one who killed him. She wanted to scratch the sneer from the guy's face.

"What do you *want*?" she hissed.

"The item your *late* husband hid." The emphasis he placed on the word showed her he wanted to hurt her.

"I don't know what you're talking about. If he hid anything, he never told me." Ahri thought frantically for something Zed could have hidden in their apartment. If it tied back to his job, it had to be information. Were they looking for a flash drive? There'd probably been a dozen of them at the house. Could that really be what they were looking for?

"I didn't bring any flash drives with me," she said.

"Ah," Rafe breathed, seeming to understand.

"You burned them all with the rest of my things in the truck." Except for her clothes and toiletries, she hadn't brought anything . . . Ahri went cold. Whatever happened, she would *not* lead them to Francie's house.

"Ah, yes, I see you've remembered something." The man's expression had gone hard, the muscles in his jaw twitching. "Hand it over."

Rafe edged in front of her.

"It must have been in my mother's doll." Ahri pulled on her high school acting abilities to sound as sincere as she could.

"That doll . . ." Rafe's words faded. He must have remembered where it was.

"Yes." Ahri forced her gaze to meet the man's. "The one I mailed back to my mother."

"*What?*" the man almost shouted. "Where?"

"Korea."

She felt the satisfaction of his jaw dropping, but it was short-lived. He studied her with growing agitation, his eyes narrowing. She thought if he didn't think he needed her, he'd shoot her right there.

"Let's go find out if you're lying." He used the gun to signal they should go through the door into Kayn's private quarters.

Rafe didn't move, his heart pounding. The man's words still echoed in his mind: *Only if you want to die right away.* Rafe's gut told him if he turned around, he'd get a bullet. The skin on his back prickled in anticipation. He was excess baggage, but the guy needed Ahri. For now.

Then she shifted her head enough for him to see her lips but still hide them from the man. She mouthed *wombo-combo*. Rafe barely had time to take in that she meant an in-game attack they used when she was his support while they played REKD.

It all seemed to happen at once. With a guttural sound, she burst forward, throwing her over-sized sword at the man, her shield held high. Surprised, their assailant ducked to the side, firing off a couple of rounds.

"Ahri," Rafe cried, his gut clenching with fear. He leapt toward them, his toy rifle over his head. Unlike the champions in his game, if they died, they wouldn't regenerate to fight again.

She slammed into the man with her shield. He fell against the hallway wall but kicked out his foot. It caught her in the side. With a cry of pain, she crashed against a display case and crumpled to the floor. The man lifted his gun to fire again.

"No!" Powered by adrenaline, Rafe brought his rifle down on the man's arm.

He grunted, and the revolver flew across the floor. Rafe tried to hit him in the face. The man dodged, clutching his injured arm to his chest. He threw an uppercut with his other hand. It grazed Rafe's jaw, making his teeth snap together. With a roar, he leaped on the man, and they went to the ground. On top of him, Rafe used his elbows and hands to punch anything he could reach.

The man arched his back, using his feet again to reverse them. Rafe smacked his head on the floor and saw stars for a second. Their assailant skittered on his hands and knees across the floor toward the gun. Rafe was staggering to his feet when Ahri got there again, holding her sword but by the blade end. She swung and struck the guy's head with the pommel. He collapsed.

Rafe lumbered to the gun and picked it up. Swaying a little, he pointed it at the man, but he wasn't moving.

Heaving out a breath, Rafe reached out to Ahri. She stumbled into his arms.

"What were you *thinking* to run at him like that?" he asked against her hair. "I thought I was going to lose you there."

"He didn't want *me* dead," She looked up at him, "and I had my armor and my shield."

"But it isn't real armor, my love."

"It's metal."

Shaking his head, Rafe pointed to where her shield lay on the floor. She gasped at the two bullet holes in it.

"He could have *killed* you," he said weakly.

"He was going to kill both of us anyway," Ahri said, her voice flat. He was glad she'd recognized that. She tried to move her left arm and let out a groan of pain.

Before he could ask her about it, an unfamiliar voice called out from Kayn's partially open suite door.

"Drop the gun."

Not again. Rafe ground his teeth as he whipped up his gun arm and pointed it at the Hispanic man's face. Ahri let out a little sob but didn't move.

"I think you'd better drop yours instead," Bill said from behind the man, who tensed. For a second Rafe thought the guy was going to fire anyway. "Don't make me shoot you." Bill had never sounded so cold.

The man heaved out a breath and let the revolver drop. He lifted his hands and placed them on top of his head, a position he seemed to know well. One of Bill's men patted him down while another one retrieved the pistol. In the distance came the sound of sirens.

Rafe handed his weapon to a third security guard and put his arms around Ahri.

"Ahri, you're *bleeding*," Kayn cried, his breaths heaving as he ran to them.

"Where?" Rafe pushed her back from him, searching her body.

"Her arm." Her brother gently pulled the wet fabric from her skin on her left arm.

"You *are*." Rafe's stomach knotted as he helped Kayn tear away the material.

"Ow." Ahri tried to pull away and moaned. "Stop poking at it."

"It looks like it's just a graze," Bill said, making her stand still. "You're lucky."

"What about Rafe?" She reached up and wiped something from his chin. "He hit you."

"You too." He ran a knuckle over the imprint of her helmet on her cheek. "You're going to have a nice bruise there."

"We need to get you two to the hospital." Kayn's face was pale.

"I'm fine," Rafe said. "I can't let those people at the banquet down. We can send Ahri—"

"No way. I have a date with the CEO." Ahri glanced at Bill. "Do I need stitches?"

"Nah. Just a good cleaning and a bandage."

"See." She stood on her tiptoes and kissed Rafe.

"I'm getting really tired of this armor," he said, when she almost spiked his chest again.

"Well," Kayn crossed his arms, grinning at them, "It's about time you two could finally get together. It's been driving me crazy watching you."

"Oh, shut up." Ahri gave him a weak grin.

"The police will need a report." Bill accepted a first aid kit from one of his men. "I don't think either of you are hurt too badly, but I'd really feel better if you were both examined by a doctor."

"What's all this?" Darius asked as he and Ezreal strode into the hallway, both dressed for the banquet.

"Ow." Ahri tried to pull away from Bill who was cleaning her wound.

"What happened to you?" Darius averted his gaze from what the security chief was doing.

"I got shot."

"*What?*" Ez was at her side in a flash, his face full of worry. "Are you all right? What can I do to help?"

"She's in good hands." Rafe clasped his friend's shoulder, glad to see his concern.

"That's going to hurt tonight. Here, let me hold the bandage." Ez put his fingers over the pad so Bill could tape it in place. "You might need something stronger than over-the-counter painkillers."

"Do you speak from experience?" Ahri winced again.

"Yeah. My brother shot me with a BB gun when I was twelve. *Man*, did that hurt."

"It's going to leave an ugly scar," she said, trying to see her arm. "See. This is why you can't show your female champs going into battle wearing skimpy clothes. All that pretty skin's going to look terrible after a few skirmishes."

"She has a point, Darius." Ez stepped back. "You should be fine once the scar's had time to fade."

"Someone's going to have to explain to our guests why the police are here," Darius said.

"I'll talk to them for now, but you'll eventually have to talk to them yourselves." Bill looked between Ahri and Rafe. "You two are sure you're all right to go to the banquet first?"

"Yes. I'm fine," Rafe said.

"I'm going with him." Ahri pointed at Rafe. "But I need to tell you something." She whispered in his head of security's ear. He then strode toward the building entrance where uniformed officers were entering, followed by his men and their prisoners. Bill's team must have wakened the first guy and cuffed them both.

"We have to get dressed," Rafe said.

"I'm guessing we'll have a really interesting Sunday dinner discussion tomorrow," Kayn said. "Let's go change."

Chapter 19

A as she tried to dress, Ahri found she couldn't move her left arm without a lot of pain, more than she thought the cut from the bullet should have caused. She also had an assortment of bruises, some of them pretty spectacular, where the guy had kicked her into the furniture. Was that when she'd hurt her shoulder?

How badly would she have been injured if she hadn't had on the armor? She'd definitely go to the ER after the banquet.

"You ready?" Kayn asked, tapping on her door.

"As good as I can get, I guess." If he knew how much she was hurting, he'd insist on taking her to the hospital, so Ahri bit back a groan as she opened the door. She raised her hands, keeping her elbows at her side. "How do I look?"

He reached over like he was going to touch her bruised cheek, but she turned her face.

"Don't mess with the concealer."

"Sorry." Kayn opened his arms. She stepped into them, only able to hug him with her right arm.

"Not too tight," she breathed when he reciprocated. "I'm stiff."

"Sorry." He released her and stepped back, his face twisted with emotion. "You might have been killed."

"But I wasn't, and now it's finally over." Ahri reached up with her good arm and patted his cheek.

"What did you tell Bill?" he asked.

"That I think Zed hid something in Mom's Korean doll. I'm guessing a flash drive."

"Oh, wow." Her brother looked at her, bemused. "If you'd have shipped it with the rest of your stuff, they'd have gotten it."

"Yeah. I called Francie before I took my shower and told her to watch for the police. It scares me to death they could have come after me there." Ahri had to blink back tears.

"It's okay. They didn't." He kissed her forehead. "Remember, it's over. You ready?"

Kayn's bell chimed at the same time the door opened. Rafe entered, dressed in a tux with a white jacket this time, and a red rose in his lapel. He looked so good, Ahri sighed.

"You have *two* tuxes?" she asked.

"The black one was my costume." He opened the box he held and pulled out a corsage. "Ahri, you look beautiful."

"More prom stuff?" Kayn didn't wait for an answer. "No PDA around me, okay? Let's go."

"Let me put on my flower." Ahri took it from Rafe but needed his help to pin it on. She faced him and whispered, "How bad do you hurt?"

"I'm going to need some time in a hot tub."

"Me too."

He kissed her, took her right hand, and led her to the banquet. When they entered the room, they found Darius welcoming the guests. He looked relieved when he saw them.

"Well, it looks like our CEO Rafe Davis has arrived. I'll turn the time over to him." As everyone clapped, Darius took a seat.

They walked to the front table together, Rafe on one side of her and Kayn on the other. Ahri didn't think it was a coincidence, and it made her feel protected. She accepted it for the kindness she was sure they meant it to be. Rafe seated her and moved to the podium.

"I'd like to welcome everyone to our first annual Midsummer's Eve Banquet. Did everyone have fun today?" The crowd erupted in applause and some cheers. When everyone quieted, he continued. "We had a little incident today—" He indicated his face. "—but rest assured that it's been resolved and the bad guys are in custody. Since it's an ongoing police investigation, we can't answer any questions, so don't ask. I'm sure everyone's ready to eat, so the service can begin."

The longer Ahri sat, the stiffer she became and the more her left shoulder ached. It didn't hurt as much if she kept her arm at her side. As often as Rafe shifted in his chair, she knew he wasn't doing much better. She didn't do the delicious meal justice.

When everyone had been served dessert, Rafe rose, moving a lot like an old man who was stiff with arthritis. He acknowledged their guests from the community, such as the university president and local elected officials and then put on a forced grin for the group.

"I'd like now to thank our guests of honor. These are people who've done the most to share their love of playing REKD. Word of mouth is everything, and your contributions have helped with our amazing success. Your efforts have grown the popularity of the game worldwide. We have a special gift for each of you, as well as a plaque like this." Rafe held one up. "These will be placed on our Wall of Honor here at headquarters."

Ahri was hurting so much by then, that she lost the rest of what he said. She only came out of her fog of pain when he put his hands on her shoulders. She looked up.

"I think we'll go to the hospital now," he said.

"What about the hospital?" Kayn was at her chair in an instant.

"I don't know if I can get up," she whispered, her voice tight with pain.

"We need to be discrete," Bill said. "Don't try to pull her up. Let her hold onto you."

Ahri took the forearm Kayn offered her. As soon as she tried to stand, a stabbing pain in her left shoulder made her cry out.

"Stop," Bill said. "If I'd seen the video of your little fight before you left for the dinner, I wouldn't have let you go. You hit that display case pretty hard. Let's wait until the last of the guests have gone."

Ahri sat while the guests filed out, unable to think of anything but the pain. It intensified when someone picked her up. Kayn. He placed her on a stretcher.

"What about Rafe?" she asked.

"He didn't get hit as hard as you did, but he's coming to the ER too," Bill said. "Don't worry."

"Rafe," she called.

"I'm here." He took her right hand.

"Tell your mother I'll be late tonight."

"She's meeting us at the hospital."

With another wave of pain, Ahri lost track of things again. Eventually, blessed relief flooded through her, and she opened her eyes to find an EMT working over her.

"I've given you some painkillers, so you should be feeling better," the man said as he adjusted an IV drip.

"I do. Thank you."

The medication made her drowsy, and she was in and out for the exam. At one point, an agonizing pain shot through her shoulder. She screamed and everything went black.

When she roused, she found herself in a different room, being transferred to a bed.

"I don't have to stay here, do I?" Ahri gasped. It was hard to breathe. The room swayed. "I can't seem to get enough air."

"That's because they gave you a nerve block for the pain in your shoulder." The male nurse sent her a sympathetic glance as he typed something into the computer. "Unfortunately, it caused your left lung to collapse. It should just be temporary, but the doctor's keeping you here for observation until the block wears off."

"I don't want to be alone," Ahri said.

"Don't worry. Your mother's here," he said.

Her mother was in Korea.

"Hey." Francie came to stand on the other side of the bed and took Ahri's hand.

Emotion stole over her, and she had to blink back tears.

"Rafe asked me to come to you while Kayn gives him some moral support." His mother's face turned troubled.

"Is he all right?"

"He's in x-ray right now." Francie looked pale and worried, but also determined. "He was bleeding from one ear, and the doctor wants to rule out a skull fracture."

Ahri's mouth went dry. Rafe *had* to be all right.

"You two don't have the brains God gave little green apples," Francie muttered in disgust, "going to the banquet instead of coming here."

"We didn't think he was hurt that bad," Ahri said.

"And he might not be," the nurse observed. "It's also a precaution. I'm going to send your friends in. It's late, so they can't stay long."

Ahri waited until he'd stepped out of the room to ask, "Did the police come to pick up my doll?"

"Yes."

"I'm so sorry." Ahri winced and put a hand to her chest, her eyes burning. "I'd never have brought it to your house if I'd known."

"Of course, you wouldn't." Francie handed over a tissue. "If you'd known, you'd have given it to the police."

The door swung open, and Kayn pushed in a wheelchair carrying Rafe. "Enter the conquering hero," her brother cried, Ezreal and Darius following.

"Shhh." Francie jumped to her feet and hurried to her son. "There are people in the other rooms trying to sleep." She gave Rafe a quick hug.

"Are you kidding?" Kayn said but more quietly. "No one can sleep in a hospital room because they're in and out all night." He bent to kiss Ahri on the forehead. "How are you?"

"It's hard to breathe." She looked at Rafe. "How are you?"

"Better than you, it appears. I get to go home tonight." When he tried to move the chair forward himself, Ez pushed it next to the bed, forcing Kayn to shift out of the way. Rafe took her hand. "I hate to leave you here alone, but they won't let me stay."

"*I'm* staying," Kayn said.

"Thank you." Rafe brought her hand to his lips.

The nurse opened the door and held it open. "Okay, everyone. You've seen she's all right. Now she needs to get some rest."

"You'll bring her to my mother's tomorrow?" Rafe asked Kayn.

"Of course."

He leaned forward as though to kiss her, but she couldn't reach him.

"*Fine.*" Rolling his eyes, Kayn helped Rafe to stand.

"I should've let Darius handle the banquet and insisted that you be seen." Rafe pressed his warm lips to hers, and he lifted her hand to the bandage on his cheek.

"I guess I'd better get used to this smoochy stuff, hadn't I?" Kayn asked.

"For your self-preservation, yes." Rafe released her hand and straightened.

"She really does need to get some rest." The nurse took the handles to the chair, and Rafe sat in it.

Francie came over to the bed and brushed a kiss on Ahri's forehead. "I'm so happy to see you and Rafe together," she whispered.

Ahri watched them leave. She felt weary and a little bemused by all that had happened that day.

"It's really still Saturday, right?" she asked her brother.

"Just barely." Kayn watched her, his gaze tender. "So, you and Rafe, huh?"

"Yeah."

"Good." He rubbed his hands together and shot her a diabolical look like he used to do when they were kids. "We'll keep all this money in the family."

"Someday you'll have a family of your own."

He made a disgusted sound. "Not me. I'm not the marrying kind. A woman needs a man who'll *be* there and not caught up in a video game, if you catch my drift."

"I'm sure there's some computer nerd out there who's as in love with programming as you are." Ahri shifted, and a twinge in her side reminded her why she was there. "I never did find out what's hurt on me."

"The doc said you bruised some ribs and partially dislocated your left shoulder," Kayn said. "I told them you've had some trouble with anesthesia. That's why they gave you that nerve block. I guess they hit something wrong, and it caused the lung thing."

"Thanks for staying tonight." She reached out a hand to him, and he took it.

"Any time, sis."

284

Epilogue

Looking out his bedroom window at the October trees, Rafe had to heave out a breath to settle his nervous stomach. He fingered the small box in his pocket. Last week had been the six-month anniversary of Zed's murder, and Rafe hoped it'd been enough time. Today's family barbecue would be the last one of the summer. It seemed the perfect time.

His mind flashed back to the night Alex had proposed to Francie. He'd taken her to a nice restaurant filled with their friends and coworkers. Rafe had come home from Harvard for it.

For himself, because he was too well known in the area, he didn't feel comfortable doing anything quite so flamboyant. Was he cheating Ahri out of that kind of memory? Or was he a coward because he was afraid she might turn him down? He didn't *think* she would. They'd dated exclusively since Midsummer's Eve and had discussed a future together.

He fingered the ring box again. More doubts assailed him. Was he being presumptuous in picking one out without her? Why could he be decisive about business-related things but second-guess every detail with Ahri?

When Rafe opened his garage door, he found the guys already waiting in the driveway.

"Everything's set up at your mother's place," Kayn said with a grin.

"Show it to us." Ez held out his hand.

Rafe pulled out the box and opened it.

"I like the simple design," Darius said. "It has style but isn't ostentatious."

"Good choice." Kayn nodded. "She's not into fancy stuff."

"Simple and beautiful, like Ahri," Ez said.

Rafe put the box back in his pocket. "Let's do this."

As they approached the B&B, Rafe could make out the first zip line platform on the tree in the distance. It'd been quite a production to get everything built and inspected for safety during the week while keeping Ahri away. His mother had taken her and the children to the outlet stores yesterday and kept them out all day.

"You sure she hasn't been to the house this week?" he asked.

"I made sure her boss knew to have lots for her to do during the day," Kayn said.

"I didn't have to make up work for her either," Darius said. "She's got your eye for detail, man. She's the best paid intern I've ever had."

"Even if she's always pushing to rework the armor on our female champions?" Rafe asked, with a chuckle.

"Well, her argument's a good one if we want to appeal to a broader audience." Darius shrugged.

Lessa and Nik burst out the front door at the sound of his car. As soon as Rafe opened his door, she ran to him carrying a bear.

"Ma said this is the best place for it because I can carry it in my harness." She held the toy out for him to examine.

"You'll have to be careful not to lose any of his stuffing." He examined where the seam had been opened.

"Ahri should be here in half an hour." His mother smiled at him. "May I look at it?"

Rafe handed her the little box. She opened it and bent over so the children could see the ring too.

"I promise I won't drop it." Lessa gave him a huge smile. "I'm going to have a *sister.*"

"If she accepts me," Rafe muttered under his breath.

"Remember, Nik, that you can*not* say anything about this to Ahri." Ma made a zipping motion across her mouth, and the little boy did the same thing.

"He's not going to last very long," Alex said, "so you'll want to do it as soon as she gets here. Lessa's been practicing all morning. She can't wait until she's ten and can go ziplining for real."

"I'll get this closed up." His mother and sister headed back inside.

"How are you holding up?" Alex asked.

"I think I'm getting an ulcer." Rafe rubbed his abdomen.

"Seeing you two together, I don't think you have anything to worry about." His stepfather clapped him on the shoulder. "I'm happy for you."

Rafe hoped the congratulations weren't premature. He went to the large tree that provided the cushioned stop for the miniature zip line. They'd patterned it off the one used for training. His mother wasn't thrilled about having it there because she was worried the kids would try to use it without supervision.

At the sound of a car, he headed back to the house. It turned out to be Lessa's piano teacher and her two children. Another car pulled up behind them, this one with Cass and her little family. When another vehicle drove into the driveway, full of Ahri's class friends, Rafe's nerves ratcheted up. He hadn't expected this large an audience.

"I thought it was just going to be the family," he said to his mother.

"This will be an important day for Ahri. You shouldn't be the only one here with family and friends around you."

"Ma, what if she says no?"

"Be brave, my sweet son." His mother patted his cheek and strode over to greet her new guests.

The next car to arrive carried Bill Ryze and his wife. Rafe had made that invitation. The police had finally released the hallway fight video, and the guys had insisted they wanted to watch it after the kids went to bed. Rafe didn't want to see it; he already had enough nightmares of it, but Ahri had said she hoped watching it would help her put it to rest. He wouldn't let her sit through it without him.

When the police had reported finding a flash drive taped underneath the dress of Ahri's Korean doll, Rafe had thought for a second that she might pass out. He'd needed both Francie and Alex's help to talk Ahri off the emotional ledge on that one. She'd tried to blame herself for putting them in danger, but Ma would have nothing of it.

Sadly, the information on the drive had confirmed that Zed had not only known he'd been helping to launder drug cartel money but had tried to steal some of it. The police could only guess the motivation, though it appeared to go back to Zed's gambling problems.

"Are you okay?" Rafe had asked Ahri when they'd hung up the phone with the police.

"Yes. I'm just sad that he wasted his life for something so stupid. It's weird. It's like I've learned this about a stranger; I feel emotionally removed from it." She'd let out a breath. "For the first time, I feel free to move on."

At the sound of a car, Rafe glanced up. Ahri. He jogged over to open her door and pull her into an embrace.

"Hey, what's that all about?" she asked when he released her.

"Just missed you yesterday." It was true. He took her hand, hoping his nerves didn't show. All night he'd had recurring nightmares that she turned him down.

"Is that a zip line?" she asked.

"It sure is."

Dressed in her harness, Lessa bounced with excitement where she and Alex stood on the platform around the tree for the zip line. Rafe gave Alex a subtle nod, and he grinned.

"Since everyone has arrived," his stepfather said, "our little lady here wants to show everyone that she's brave like her mother."

"Did you arrange this?" Ahri whispered to Rafe.

"Me and the guys." His heart was thudding so hard he was sure she must hear it. Was he giving it away? "It's all she's talked about since we went without her."

"You ready?" Alex asked after he made sure Lessa's hands were solidly on the brake. She nodded, and he gave her a gentle push off the platform.

Rafe's little sister squealed all the way to the end where he'd positioned himself and Ahri.

"You brave girl!" Ahri said, steadying her.

Without looking at him, Lessa pulled the bear from her harness. Everyone edged closer, and Rafe waited for Ahri to see the opening in the toy.

"Inside. Inside," Nik said, pointing.

Ahri's brows quirked up, and she seemed unsure what she was supposed to do.

"Take it out," Lessa cried, and Nik added, "Yes, take it out."

As Ahri put her fingers inside and pulled out the box, Rafe dropped to one knee. She gasped, and her eyes immediately filled with tears. For the first time, a sense of peace washed over him, and he took her hand.

"Sweet Ahri, I've felt a pull to you since the first time we met. It's only gotten stronger the more I've learned about you. I've told you before that I love you. I want to spend the rest of my life with you. Will you marry me?"

She put her hands to her mouth and dropped the ring box. Kayn was close enough to catch it. Laughing, he handed it to Rafe. He opened it and took out the ring.

"If you don't like it, we can go ring shopping. The important question is, do you want this too? Do you want *us*?" Holding up the ring expectantly, he waited, his hands cold. Except for the birds in the trees and a slight rustle of the leaves, there was silence around them. He'd never felt so exposed in his life.

Ahri wiped at her eyes and reached for his hand. When she tightened hers over his, closing his fingers around the ring, his breath caught. *Was* she going to turn him down?

Then she was putting pressure on his hand to stand.

"Come *on*," Kayn hissed. "Stop toying with the man."

Ahri shot her brother a dark look and pulled Rafe to his feet. "Bill, aren't Rafe and I one of the best bottom lane teams?"

"After watching you two fight in that footage," the security chief said with a chuckle, "I don't think there's anything that can beat the two of you together."

"Oh, Rafe. With you I'm finally home. Of *course*, I'll marry you."

Everyone seemed to release a collective breath.

Ahri held out her left arm, and with shaking hands, Rafe slid the ring on her third finger. She slid her arms around his neck and kissed him.

The crowd let loose, and everyone was trying to hug them.

I love you, he mouthed.

The blaze in her eyes sent fire through him and with it came a sense that he was enough. *More* than enough.

The End

Turn the page to find out how to receive the **FREE** book Hope's Watch, Safe Harbors #1.5.

Author's Note
& a Free Book

Dear Reader,

Thank you for taking the time to read *Hiding with the Billionaire*. There are so many book options out there that I feel privileged you chose my book.

If you enjoyed it, I would be thrilled to have you leave a review on Goodreads or Amazon or anywhere else you share your thoughts on books.

I also love to hear from readers. You can find me on Facebook, Twitter, my blog at donnakweaver.com, or you can email me at donnakweaver@gmail.com.

Thanks!
Donna

Receive the **FREE** book Hope's Watch, Safe Harbors #1.5 and updates on new releases by typing this link into your browser: https://goo.gl/4ZcuG5

Hope's Watch

Book 1.5 in the *Safe Harbors* Series

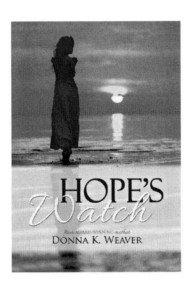

HOPE'S
Watch
From AWARD-WINNING author
DONNA K. WEAVER

Elle Reinhardt is filled with emotional wounds from a ship excursion gone wrong that ended in death and disaster at the hands of modern-day pirates. As grieving loved ones wait for news of those lost at sea, she tries desperately to buoy them up.

Malcolm Armstrong, friend of one of the missing men, arrives to act as family spokesman. Elle knows it's unreasonable, but she resents his presence. When Mal offers the strength she so desperately needs, will she be able to let go of her animosity and accept his support?

This ebook novelette includes excerpts from both *A Change of Plans* and *Torn Canvas*.

About the Author

Award-winning author, wife, mother, grandmother, Army veteran, karate black belt, Harry Potter nerd, online gamer.

Books by Donna K. Weaver
Available in Audio, Print, and eBook

The *Safe Harbors* Series
A Change of Plans (#1)
Hope's Watch (#1.5)
Torn Canvas (#2)
A Season of Change (#2.5)
Swing Vote (#3)
Kings Crossed Lovers (#4)

Ripple Effect Romance Novella (#5) Series
Second Chances 101

Twickenham Time Travel Romances
Against the Magic
With the Magic (coming 2019)

Billionaires of REKD Series
Hiding with the Billionaire (#1)
The Billionaire's Masterpiece (#2)

Solo Titles
Teapots & Treachery

Acknowledgements

No book is ever written alone, even though it might seem that way as I sit in my office writing away. My wonderful husband Edward is the best support any author could as for.

My critique partners are fabulous in taking time and offering me great feedback to make a better story, and I thank Canda, Alison, Meredith, and Rynn. And I so appreciate the guidance from my editor Katharina Brendel.

And I appreciate my "friends" in the online gaming world who help me to relax in "battles." Learning new things and forcing me to improve helps to keep the gray matter working in this old lady. Some of my most enjoyable evenings are ones spent queuing up with my husband and son(s) for a few games.

27416059R00186

Made in the USA
Columbia, SC
24 September 2018